DESERT NURSE

After the break-up of her romance with Greg
Ryder, Nurse Martha Shore decided to get away
from it all by accepting Doctor Jude Tarleton's
offer of a post in his tiny hospital east of Aden.
She had successfully jumped out of the frying-
pan. Was her new job, in the burning desert heat,
not ominously like the proverbial fire?

DESERT NURSE

BY

JANE ARBOR

MILLS & BOON LIMITED
17–19 FOLEY STREET
LONDON W1A 1DR

First published *1963*
This edition *1974*

© *Jane Arbor 1963*

ISBN 0 263 716074

*Made and Printed in Great Britain by
C. Nicholls & Company Ltd
The Philips Park Press, Manchester*

CHAPTER I

"Ah, Dr. Tarleton – do come in." Grace Armour, Matron of the Bexham Cottage Hospital, rose to greet the man whom an orderly was showing into the sitting room of her private quarters, then turned to introduce the girl seated behind her.

Her extended hand linked them. "Dr. Tarleton, this is Miss Shore. Martha dear – Dr. Jude Tarleton, Bonny Tarleton's brother. As I told you, Doctor, Martha only arrived this morning before lunch. But I've briefed her a little. So as I'm due at a Hospital Finances meeting which will keep me until around five, I must leave the two of you to talk things over without me. I think you said, didn't you, that you must get away by four or so."

Her visitor nodded. "In time to catch the four-thirty back to London, yes."

"That's what I thought. However, perhaps we can hope to see you again before you leave England? You'd be very welcome, you know, for your sister's sake as well as your own."

A moment's hesitation at that. Then: "You are more than kind, Matron, but I think not."

"Then if this must be goodbye, you know you take all my good wishes away with you?"

"I'm very sure of that. Meanwhile, thank you for everything."

Grace Armour shook her white-coifed head. "Please! So little, so pitifully little to do for Bonny," she

5

murmured as she went out of the door which Jude Tarleton opened for her.

Meanwhile Martha had been appraising the looks of the man who – just possibly – might be her future chief, noticing his broad-shouldered bulk, his ease of manner, his good voice; liking the capable look of his hands as much as she did the frank deep-set stare of his eyes, though aware that she would not care to meet it in any professional difference in which he might be right and she in the wrong. . . .

Also, in the minute or two of his sitting down opposite to her, she tried to see herself through his eyes by the same mental check as she had applied to him.

Hands – well cared for and equal to all her work demanded of them. Eyes – greyish-green beneath brows rather too fair for her liking, though their colouring was all of a piece with that of her hair, curved forward at each temple and swathed into a neat French twist from crown to nape. Features – nothing remarkable. Figure – satisfactorily slim in the square-necked dress of her travelling three-piece. Voice – but who was ever able to judge their own voice? was her final thought before her companion spoke.

"Well now, suppose I recap on what I know of you?" he suggested "You're twenty-six, I think? You are fully qualified and C.M.B. At your late hospital you've been staff nurse for two years and as yet you have nothing else in view. Now, what were your reasons for resigning from – what was it – Meerstead General, when surely your next logical step up would have been into a ward of your own?"

It was a question she had known she must expect and she was prepared for it. "I had trained at Meerstead, and I had decided that a total of over six years in one hospital was enough," she told him.

6

"I see." Appearing satisfied with the evasion of the truth which that was, he went on, "You've done no professional nursing here under Miss Armour?"

"Not officially. As I daresay she has told you, she has made a home here for me since before I left school. I've spent nearly all my leaves here, and between school and my being accepted at Meerstead I used to work on the wards as a kind of dogsbody, and loved it. But that's all."

"Yes, that's roughly what I had gathered. You became Miss Armour's ward after your own parents died?"

Martha corrected, "There again, not officially. But Grace – Miss Armour – was my mother's best friend. They had trained together in nursing, and when my mother died six years before my father, I used to spend one school holiday a year with him out in Aden and the other two here."

"Since when you haven't been again to the Middle East? Still, you probably know something about the conditions, the people, the climate. Did you manage to pick up any Arabic, by the way?"

Martha smiled. "A little. But it's pretty rusty now."

"Right. So that's your background. Now for mine, on which I daresay Miss Armour may have briefed you?"

Martha told him yes. For she knew from Grace of the tragedy which had coincided with his return from Saudi Arabia on a rare leave; of his intention to take back with him his sister Bonny as nurse to the clinic he ran in an up-country outpost peopled only by semi-nomad Bedouins, a number of European geologists and engineers engaged in sounding for oil, and his own small medical staff; of how Bonny, for three years a ward sister here at Bexham, had volunteered for isolation duty in an area gripped by smallpox, only to contract it herself and to die almost to the hour of her brother's homecoming aircraft touching down. At a loss for words which would not be a trite echo of everyone else's sympathy, Martha added simply, "I knew Bonny too, you know, Dr. Tarleton. We only met when I've been back on leave here. But somehow I always felt privileged in knowing her even so little. She was such a complete, serene person. More than happy – so fulfilled and utterly content."

"Thank you, though I think you needn't look far for the reason. For Bonny, nursing had always had all the answers," Jude Tarleton agreed. He squared his shoulders as if the movement helped to ease the yoke of an intolerable memory. He went on, "So this brings us to where we came in – to Miss Armour's suggestion that in view of your existing links with my part of the world, you might be interested in taking Bonny's place?"

"I think I might be – very," Martha said.

"So – the geography is roughly this — " On a memo pad he drew briefly, then turned it towards her to show a just recognizable outline of Southern Arabia. His pencil stabbed. "Aden here. Over here" – another stab – "is Taroued, our base, about a hundred miles inland from Bab Magreb, our nearest fair-sized town and port. Taroued – is your rusty Arabic equal to 'oued'?"

"I think it means a long-dry watercourse or river bed, doesn't it?"

"Yes. The 'Tar' refers to the Tarjol, the range of mountains behind us, where there are springs which the oil people's sappers have tapped to bring us water for drinking and bathing."

"And Taroued is by way of being a village?"

"Nothing so homely, I'm afraid. If the oilmen find on the scale they hope, it could prove another Kuwait. But at present it's a huddle of mud and wooden houses; some tents on the outskirts; prefabs for the oil wallahs

8

and us; a mosque which looks as if someone had flung it at the mountain side, hoping it would cling there; and the makings of a hospital. So far we have the building, a clinic-cum-first-aid post, a path lab and a men's ward, though not yet a women's, and no nursing staff."

"No women's ward and *no* staff?" puzzled Martha.

"No. By local custom, any men in-patients bring along a member – or several – of their families to look after them. We have to treat the women in their homes under chaperonage, and any Europeans who go sick we ward in their billets or take them down to the hospital in Bab Magreb by jeep or air. That's another thing – there's a landing strip of sorts."

"But how can you run even a men's ward without any nursing staff?"

"A good question! We can't any longer, and the idea was that Bonny, as the nucleus of it, would have trained some of the girls from the Bedouin Orphan School in Bab Magreb. Meanwhile there are only two other English-women in Taroued. Under their contract the oilmen are single or grass widowers, but there's not the same rule for medicos, and my colleague, Ben Randall, brought back a wife from his last leave in Beirut. Then there's Naomi Troy, his assistant in the lab. She is Aden born, and has been with us since Dorrit Randall's arrival made it possible to engage a woman for her job. So there's the set-up. Any other questions?"

Martha said slowly, "I'm still not sure I understand the 'why' of a hospital in such a small community as Taroued sounds."

"No? Well, the 'why' of it is that it's one of a few pilot schemes between Aden and the Persian Gulf, for the purpose of fighting at source the unnecessary killers like malnutrition and childbirth, and the real ones like malaria and bilharzia and cholera. And the particular 'how' of Taroued is thanks to the oilmen."

"How to them?"

"Because the Company had to lay on a medical service for the men on the site, so it's financing us for the period of its concession, making a permanency of the arrangement when they find oil on a commercial scale. Meanwhile the concession has twelve months yet to run, and if you want the job, you understand that I should expect you to sign on for that year?"

"Yes, I'd agree to do that."

"Good. But I should also expect more. I want to know that you would be prepared to devote yourself wholly to the idea and purpose of Taroued while you're there. In other words, that you would go facing completely towards it, not feeling still half tied to your life here. To, for instance, any unfinished romantic business like an engagement or a courtship in active eruption which could play a disastrous game of Pull Devil, Pull Baker with your work. Well? Can you give me that assurance?" Jude Tarleton asked.

Martha did not hesitate. "That I'm not engaged nor thinking of marriage? Yes."

"Nor going out with a calculating eye on the marriage-market potential of an almost entirely male world?"

She was aware of colour flooding up from her throat. "I've been nursing for six years," she reminded him. "I chose it as a career, not a-hunting-ground, and I don't think I've used it as one yet."

His faint smile was conciliatory. "I'm sorry. But the cap might have fitted. And one last point – I could also hope you wouldn't be making use of Taroued as an escape route from some romantic affair which had gone sour on you? Because frankly I don't want you there if you were."

There was a beat of silence. Then Martha said,

choosing her words, "If you offered me the job, Dr Tarleton, you could take it that I shouldn't merely be escaping into it from any situation that I'd failed to handle here."

His eyes met hers levelly. "Thank you. I have your word for that – and the rest?"

"Yes," said Martha. And saying it, was grateful that an assurance which should have stabbed her conscience had, suddenly and incredibly, lost some of its guilt.

For though, in leaving Meerstead, she had indeed been running headlong from love, from the very thought and sight and memory of it, she had known as she spoke that she was not seeing Taroued as a bolthole but as a door to a future she could not, must not deny.

Yet, told in answer to that pointblank question, the lie remained a lie, and later she had more than one bad misgiving over it.

Ashamed of it, she did not confide its telling to Grace, and when Jude Tarleton wrote to confirm her appointment, Grace was so glad for her that it was unthinkable then to admit to that slurring of the truth. But though she knew she was sheltering behind the odds against ever being called to account over it, increasingly during the three weeks before she left England, she was able to recapture and justify the reasoning which had gone to it.

Then it seemed less important than her conviction that she must, *must* snatch the chance to do well by Taroued; less important too, for some reason, than her urge to prove herself in Jude Tarleton's eyes, to measure up somewhere near to Bonny. And now, journey's end only a few hours ahead, her conscience had abandoned the lie to oblivion. It couldn't catch up with her now.

Jude Tarleton had returned to Taroued before her, so that she was travelling alone as far as Bab Magreb, where his final letter of directions for her flight had told her she would be met. At Bab Magreb she was the only European among the handful of passengers who alighted from the small aircraft on to a defective tarmac, from the searing, bubbling heat of which it was sheer bliss to gain the relative sanctuary of the parched lawn surrounding the terminal and then the cool shuttered twilight of the waiting room.

She stood a little uncertainly, wondering who had been deputed to meet her; hoping she would be given time to freshen up before the long trek by road to Taroued. Then, behind her, a voice she recognized spoke her name, and she turned to face Jude Tarleton himself.

He greeted her, asking about the flight, told her they ought to be on their way in half an hour if they were to reach Taroued by dusk. Meanwhile he would see her luggage loaded on to his car and would have some iced coffee ordered by the time she returned from the cloak-room.

At first they drove along the coast in sight of Bab Magreb's small harbour where a couple of cargo vessels were unloading at the quay and a scattering of fishing caravels lazily rode the steel-blue bay. They by-passed the town itself, turning inland by way of a bamboo-fringed road, the surface of which deteriorated steadily from closely compacted rubble to a mere chaos of tyre tracks in shallow sand.

For twenty miles or so there were still crops – dusty date palms, bananas and green wheat, villages of unfired brick-and-mud houses, and a procession of travellers by foot, mule and ancient car on their plodding way to or from the bazaars of Bab Magreb. Then gradually there was no more cultivation, no more passers-by or laden animals, nor even the dry rustle of bamboo. Only now for mile on mile a monotonous brown terrain dotted with thorn and scrub and prickly pear, the ill-defined road stretching ahead and a horizon half obscured by the heat haze which danced tirelessly above it.

Once a gazelle started suddenly into life and raced parallel with the car for a long way. And once Martha's attention was directed far to the right by her companion's pointing finger until he said quietly:

"O.K. You can 'eyes front' again now. I was only putting up a smokescreen, not wanting you to spot an ibex carcase back there, with the vultures beginning to queue up for lunch."

"Oh!" Involuntarily she swivelled in her seat and looked back, only to find his hand firmly on the point of her shoulder, turning her forward.

"Forget it," he advised. "You'll see enough of that kind of thing in time. It's an ugly face of Arabia, just as that young gazelle was an enchanting one, but it has a hundred others. Tell me, how does it strike you after – what is it? – six years' absence?"

Martha confirmed, "Rather more than six, and then I didn't see much more than the European quarters of Aden; nothing inland, nor as far east as this."

"And did you suffer any nostalgia for it when you must have thought you mightn't come out again?"

"Yes, always. For the very smell and sound of it; the cosmopolitan-ness – is that a word? – of Aden, even for the appalling heat and the nights – especially the nights. The warm black velvet of them, and the stars—— On one or two summer nights when it was very clear, I saw the Southern Cross from the Aden cliffs."

"And apart from star-gazing, how many of the other night attractions of Aden were you allowed to sample?"

She smiled. "Not as many as I should have liked. European parties mostly – oh, what's that?"

"That" was ahead by fifty yards or so – a fortress-like

building of sandstone, totally unexpected in the arid desolation which surrounded it. Jude Tarleton slowed the car as they approached it.

"It's a resthouse, a guard post – something over our halfway mark. You'll be able to stretch your legs and we can get some Arab-fashion food here," he said. A long blast on his klaxon had the delayed effect of swinging open the big gates of an archway, and they drove past a guard into a courtyard where the official in charge of the post came to meet them.

"*Fadal. Beit beitish, o Tabib.*" He gave Martha's companion the "Come in. My house is your house" greeting which she understood, and the men talked in Arabic for some minutes while the older one eyed her curiously and made expansive gestures towards her. Then, smiling and nodding, he led the way up a stone staircase to a large whitewashed room where, in an incredibly short time, a meal of spiced lean mutton and rice, followed by dates and coffee, was served to them.

Their host watched them eat and went out with them to see them off when they were ready to leave an hour later. To his patent satisfaction money passed between Jude Tarleton and himself, and as the car moved off he addressed Martha directly for the first time.

Salaam aleikum, o Tabiba. After a moment for mental translation she puzzled aloud, "He said, 'Peace be with you, woman doctor,' didn't he? Why?"

Jude Tarleton shrugged. "My fault, do you mind? It seemed the simplest way to describe your function as my colleague and my equal. Especially as previously he had asked whether he had to congratulate me, whether you were my newly acquired 'house' – "

"Your – house?" In the instant of her grasp of the meaning of that she flushed, and he threw her an amused glance.

"I see you understand the Arabic use of 'house' to describe a wife," he said. "So as I had to repudiate you as my bride I settled for promoting you to '*tabiba*' instead. Nurse. Woman doctor. Out here it's a small distinction that isn't going to worry anyone, and as you'll be second in command to myself and Ben Randall, Taroued will think of you as *tabiba* anyway."

Silence ensued for a while after that. The car ate up the miles, and Martha, soothed by the steady hum of its engine, was near to drowsiness when, suddenly though casually, her companion asked,

"Tell me, why did you lie to me when I interviewed you for the job?"

For a moment it was as if she had taken a physical blow somewhere beneath her heart, and the cruel pulse of shock left her sick, winded and unable to reply until he glanced at her inquiringly and invited, "Well?"

Even then – "Wh–why did I lie?" was all she managed to falter.

"Well, you did, didn't you?" His tone was even, almost incurious.

She braced herself. "Yes. How did you know?"

"Through Miss Armour."

"Through —— ? *Grace* told you?"

A brief nod. "She wrote to me before I left England about some affairs of Bonny's. She assured me that in her opinion, failing Bonny, I couldn't have done better than to select you, and said how grateful she was that, through the job, you would have the chance to escape from and forget a love affair which had used you pretty badly."

Martha drew a long tremulous breath. "Oh, she shouldn't have! And she didn't tell me she had written to you!"

"You shouldn't blame her. She wasn't betraying you.

She wrote, meaning a kindness towards you in asking my sympathy for you, I daresay. She couldn't know I had made an issue of your word that you wouldn't be bringing any concentration-sapping distractions with you. And it could have occurred to you that there were other ways in which I could have checked on you. For in-stance, through taking up your Meerstead references."

"I suppose I thought Matron there would only tell you I was leaving because I wanted a change, which was the truth."

"Which was all I did hear from her, as it happened. But as a committed liar, you shouldn't have banked on it. So now perhaps you'll tell me why you saw fit to mislead me?"

Martha hesitated. "I don't know how to explain it. I did understand you needed to know you would be getting my – or anyone's – whole heart for the job. And I wanted it so much, felt sure I could do it, if only you would give me the chance. So, when you said you wouldn't, if I were cluttered by – other things on my mind, then I lied, telling myself I was justified. That – that's all there was to it, I'm afraid."

Another nod appeared to accept that. "I see. You weren't giving me credit for being able to weigh the thing on its merits? All right. But now we'll clear our decks, shall we? All I heard from Miss Armour was that you had been thrown over by a man at Meerstead, but she left your late fiancé faceless and nameless, and I didn't mention the subject when I wrote back to her. So go ahead now. What were the circumstances?"

"Well, my fiancé's name was Ryder, Greg Ryder——"

"On the staff at Meerstead?"

"No. His father was the senior orthopaedic consultant there, but Greg wasn't in medicine. He had had a short-service commission in the R.A.F. But he was living at home while he looked for a job which appealed to him. I met him at a hospital dance. We were engaged a year."

"And he was looking for a suitable job all that time?"

"Oh no." Instinctively Martha defended Greg against the tone of the question. "He did some civil flying for a while, and when we – we broke up he was considering going into partnership in charter work."

"And why did he break with you?"

"For one of the more usual reasons. He fell in love with someone else and asked me to release him."

"Did you know the other girl?"

"Yes. She lived in Meerstead too. She was the daughter of the man who would be sponsoring and financing the charter company for his son and Greg."

"H'm. A family affair. So you duly released this character at his request? How long then before you left Meerstead?"

"Only a very short while. I gave in my notice almost at once and left as soon as I had worked it out. That was a day or two before I came back to Bexham and you interviewed me."

"Wasn't that throwing in the sponge a shade too readily?"

"What else could I do?" The small gesture of her hand was resigned. "I – loved Greg, but when he didn't want *me* any longer my whole instinct was to run away as fast and as far as I could. And while I stayed I was only an – embarrassment to him."

She saw Jude Tarleton's jaw set momentarily. "He made that clear to you?" he asked.

"He didn't have to. I knew I couldn't bear to stay, and, loving him as I did, I thought the least – and last – I could do for him was to make things as easy for him as I could. So I got out."

"And into your present job under what, if I chose, I could regard as false pretences," her companion commented dryly.

Feeling very small, Martha said nothing. Then, "Yes," she agreed. "But you shouldn't need reminding, Dr Tarleton, that whether or not it remains my present job rests with you. If you wish, and as soon as I can make the necessary arrangements, I can go back to England at my own expense."

He shook his head. "*Oh* no! I brought you out here with my eyes open, and although your pride may need to make a face-saving gesture of that sort, it had better forget it. I needed to get the thing straight, to find out what made your reasoning tick to the tune of that point-blank deception. But you're here now for the term of your contract, and it's up to you to prove to me as well as to yourself that you've got what it takes to cope with what Taroued is going to ask of you." He paused, then pointed ahead. "The Tarjol is in front of us now. We don't cross it; Taroued is tucked in under it on this side. Only a few more miles to go and we'll be there."

Martha looked, to see that the whole horizon had become a wall of mountains, their tops ridged, cliffed, but their mass a dark blue silhouette without detail against the rays of the setting sun. Beyond them, he had said, they did not go. So this was journey's end – or nearly. But before they reached it she had to know one thing.

Not looking at Jude Tarleton but at the earliest star to hang in the paling sky, she said, "You knew, before you left England, that I had lied to you. So why did you let me come?"

She had to wait for his reply. When it came – "Suppose we agree it was because you had a smattering of Arabic, when efficient nurses with more than a tongueful of schoolroom French, if as much, don't come all that

18

thick on the ground?" he offered easily.

Just that. No more, his tone making it plain that it was his final dismissal of the subject. And though she could not have said what more or less she had expected, somehow her relief was touched with disappointment.

CHAPTER II

With the setting of the sun behind the Tarjol the swift dark of the East had almost fallen by the time they exchanged the greyish-white scree of the open road for the scarcely better surface of Taroued's lanes and its central square where few men and no women lingered and the market booths were all shuttered for the night.

Jude Tarleton drove straight across this and beyond it for some distance, finally turning into a "street" of squat, prefabricated houses, in that setting as incongruous as their neat, homely English appearance was reassuring.

"Could be the newer suburbia, couldn't it?" he quipped. "Anyway, these are our quarters and the oilmen's; mod cons – with limitations, and some people, as you see, manage to scratch themselves a garden of sorts. This one is mine——" Waving a hand – "that's the Randalls'. Bonny would have dug in with me, of course. But you'll be sharing with Naomi – here."

As he spoke and stopped the car, a light flicked on in the little house and a woman's figure was silhouetted in the open doorway.

"That's Naomi. Go and introduce yourself, will you, while I bring in your bags," he added, and Martha obeyed.

Naomi Troy was slim and very dark, her skin a deep glowing bronze, her blue-black hair a thick swathe on the top of her head. She was, Martha's intuition told her, one of the rare people who never put a foot wrong in the matter of clothes. Tonight she wore scarlet lounging pants and sleeveless shirt; her bare feet in matching sandals, her only ornament an outsize ring on a fore-finger. She used exaggerated hornrims which she re-moved as Martha approached, and as Martha's hand was taken in a cool, long-fingered grip, the other girl's dark velvet eyes met hers, appraising her in return.

Naomi Troy said, "So you've arrived. We're to be housemates. But of course you'll have heard that, and that my name is Troy – Naomi Troy. I'm Ben Randall's dogsbody in the lab." Looking beyond and above Martha's head, she addressed Jude Tarleton. "You'll come in for a drink, Jude? After that, what's the pro-gramme?"

He set down Martha's cases and straightened. "I won't wait, thanks. At the moment my top priority is a bath. So if you'll give me an hour and have a meal yourselves, I suggest you both stroll along to my place later and we'll open a bottle there. Ben and Dorrit will look in, and probably Russell and Dumont and one or two others. Or would you" – he added directly to Martha – "prefer to postpone getting acquainted with the personnel until tomorrow?"

"Oh no, I'd like to come," she said.

When he had gone Naomi showed her their quarters – the lounge with a dining-corner which they would share, the tiny kitchen and laundry where their Bedouin maid, Saluma, cooked and washed, and their bedrooms, each with its minute bathroom, no bigger than a large cup-board. All the floors were tiled, with rush mats as a small concession to comfort; the furnishing was of the barest minimum, the whole place as severely functional and, according to Naomi, as like to its fellows as the proverbial peas in a pod.

Their tour ending in the room that was to be Martha's, Naomi asked if she would like a drink first or to take a bath. Martha chose the latter, only too thankful to strip down and to revel in the luxury of the tepid shower before changing into a white linen dress and sandals and going to join Naomi in the living room.

Naomi, a cigarette between the fingers of a hand which also held a glass, was executing a few desultory steps to the final notes of a dance tune on the radio. It was followed by the gabble of an announcement, and as Naomi switched off and poured a long drink Martha chose, Martha said, "You should have left it on. I'm supposed to have to practise my Arabic. Where does it come from, by the way?"

"Where does what—— ? Oh, the broadcast? From Aden."

"You're from Aden yourself, aren't you?" Martha asked.

"Yes." Naomi stubbed her cigarette, lit another. "What on earth brought *you* out here?"

Martha carefully spoke her prepared piece. "I'd been out to Aden several times while I was at school, and when I had done six years' training and ward work in the same hospital, I wanted a change. So when Dr Tarleton offered me this job in his sister's place, I took it," she said.

"Some change! You must be a glutton for it. Did you know Jude already?"

"No. Only Bonny, and her not very well." Martha explaine d her acquaintanceship with Bonny Tarleton and then countered, "What about yourself? Why did you come here?"

Naomi shrugged. "I was being badly bored in a dispensary in Aden and Jude made rather a thing of wanting me. Besides, all this concentrated he-male atmosphere and dedication intrigued me. I thought it might be amusing to find out whether they were all as monastic as Jude claimed."

"And have you found out?" Martha asked dryly.

"That'd be telling. And from time to time I have to lay on a front of dedication myself. Jude made it clear he wouldn't stand for less, and if it meant the difference between getting the job and keeping it or not, it seemed a pity to remind him of a Latin tag we learned at school – something about Nature and a hayrake. Do you know it?"

Martha nodded. "Yes, a quotation. We learned it too. Only it was a pitchfork, not a hayrake. It began '*Naturam furca expellas*' – 'You may drive out Nature with a pitchfork. But she will still return to her own'."

"That's the one. But only a fool would quote it at Jude Tarleton when he's riding his illusion that this men-without-women thing can be forced to work." Naomi yawned and set down her glass. "Would you like the other half, or shall we tell Saluma we'll eat now?" she asked.

They dined on a rather leather-textured omelette, followed prosaically by tinned pineapple chunks. "Saluma, left to herself, would feed us on kebabs and cous-cous at every meal, so stuff out of tins is a must," Naomi explained. But the black coffee was excellent, and did much to dispel the drowsiness which Martha had been fighting since she arrived.

Afterwards they walked the few yards to Jude Tarleton's bungalow, meeting Dr Randall and his wife bound on the same errand.

Naomi introduced them. Ben Randall was blue-eyed, freckled, and wore a beard. With regard to Dorrit, only her married status could make her a chaperon for the two other girls. For she was much younger than either of them – a mere child. Martha judged, of about nineteen, still puppy-plump and rather gauche, and, as her offhand greeting to Naomi revealed, lacking the poise which could have hidden her hostility towards the older girl.

Other guests at Jude Tarleton's were there before them. Without catching all their names Martha met variously the French manager of the base camp supplying gear and food stocks to the exploration camps scattered about the desert, a couple of the air pilots who flew the Company's planes, the chief seismologist, a taciturn Scot, and his son who, when the talk ceased to be general, cornered Martha and shared with her his fiery enthusiasm for his hitherto thankless job of sounding for oil where no oil appeared to be.

He explained the technicalities of seismic work. "We go out in teams, plotting stretches of fifty miles or so each, and working inward back to camp from the furthest point. We used to detonate explosives to get our soundings, but now we carry gear on a truck which drops a weight of around three tons from a height of ten feet above the ground, and as you may imagine, that gives a sizeable shock on a seismometer."

"And what does it tell you when it does?" asked Martha.

"What the underground structure is; just what is at what level; whether or not we're on to an anticline – that's a formation like an upturned saucer beneath which oil is trapped."

"But you haven't found yet?"

Nick Murray grinned. "Good for you! You're getting the jargon already. No, so far we've only tapped water, darned useful though that is. But if we don't within our deadline, I'm afraid Taroued will have had it,

24

as far as we're concerned."

"By your deadline do you mean the year your concession still has to run? But wouldn't your Company renew it if you hadn't found oil before then?"

"It probably would – if opportunity weren't a fine thing. But the local Sheikh of the whole area who grants the concession has a weather eye to the main chance, and he isn't going to waste much time in throwing us out and putting up his price to the next lot of hopefuls who happen along."

Martha thought that out. "Then if you have to go, the hospital —— ?" she began.

Nick shrugged. "I suppose it will have to fold, if we cut our losses and move on. Hard on Jude Tarleton, though. He's heart and soul with the hospital thing, and I wouldn't know what he would use for money to keep it going if we packed in——Hullo, what's up? He's leaving us. For keeps, one wonders, or is he coming back? Bad show, breaking up his own party. Hi there, Jude, whither away so fast?"

Jude Tarleton turned at the door where he had been speaking to the Arab who had served drinks and who had brought him a murmured message. "It's a duty call," he told Nick, adding to the others, "Sorry, folks. Stay as long as you like, but I may not be back. Ben—— ?"

Ben Randall put down his glass with a grimace. "Yes, Chief?"

"I shall want you. And Naomi—— Or no——" Their host's eye swept his guests, selected Martha. "You, I think. You've got to make your début some time, so you'd better come along." His forefinger indicated her glass. "What have you had to drink, by the way?"

"Not to worry. To my certain knowledge she's made one sherry last her the whole evening!" That was Nick Murray answering for her, and the other man nodded.

25

"Fair enough. Are you ready? You needn't go back and change. We can fit you up with overalls at the hospital." He led the way out to his car where a man in the swathed headdress of a Bedouin was already in the seat beside the driver's and Ben Randall was waiting to get in.

"Shall I drive, or will you?" Ben asked.

"You can, while I brief Martha. The hospital first, then the Quarter. Youssif will direct you. And step on it, man. Youssif could be dramatizing the urgency, but I think not."

On the way Jude Tarleton gave Martha the facts of the case.

"Youssif is a camel-driver and the patient is his wife who is in labour for the sixth time, having lost all the other babies. But that's no unusual pattern, and at least, this time, I've been able to give her some antenatal care, if not enough. So, though I'm expecting to have to do a Caesarian on a table by lantern-light, hampered by most of her female relations, before morning there should be a young Youssif or a Fatima with a slightly better chance of survival than the others."

"And you can't move the mother into hospital?" Martha asked.

"No. We've got to hasten slowly, and it's a minor triumph that Youssif is allowing two male doctors to attend his house. Yes, Ben, what was that?"

Ben Randall spoke over his shoulder. "I said it was a shade hard on Martha, putting her on call on her very first night. Why didn't you bring Naomi instead?"

"For one thing, because it's Martha's job. Naomi is a research chemist, not a theatre nurse. For another, Naomi hadn't made one drink enough for the evening."

"Well, for the record, nor had I," retorted Ben. "Nor, as far as I know, had you."

"And at that, how wrong can you get?," retorted his chief coolly. "On the fifty-fifty chance that Youssif would be needing me tonight, I'd stuck to tonic water." As he spoke the car drew up at the long, low mass of a building which Martha judged to be the hospital, and he was giving crisp orders to each of them in turn.

"Martha, you can stay where you are. Ben, take Youssif with you. He can help to carry the gear." He himself unlocked a door in a windowless wall and went in, followed by the other two men and leaving Martha to the darkness and silence about her.

Ben. Naomi. Jude. Martha. Used as she was to the strict etiquette of hospital, she had been surprised by the easy currency of first names here. But she liked it, she knew. Somehow, by cutting across the formalities, it made of them a team, a pattern into which she already felt herself knitted, useful, welcome.

Jude. She wondered why she should find her chief's name coming the least readily to her tongue. "Jude." She had to practise it aloud, in readiness for using it as casually as the others did; as easily as its owner called her "Martha" already and still, somehow, kept his distance as her chief.

A quarter of an hour later they left the car at the entrance to a narrow cul-de-sac and went the rest of the way on foot by the light of Jude's powerful torch, with Youssif as their guide.

Their destination was a two-storied house where a hobbled mule and roosting hens stirred on the ground floor as they crossed it and where the first-floor room into which they were shown was a fog of lamp smoke and steam through which it was barely possible to discern the young mother-to-be, fully dressed and heavily swathed in blankets in a foot-high bed in one corner.

As Jude had warned, she was surrounded by a huddle

of Bedouin women who chattered excitedly as the European party entered but who gave not an inch until Jude spoke crisply in Arabic to Youssif and the latter shepherded all but the patient's mother and his own mother from the room. Then Ben Randall busied himself with his apparatus; an operating table was improvised from the plank bed supported on trestles brought from the hospital; Jude examined and gave the girl a pre-medication, and Martha, in theatre gown and mask like the two men, prepared sterile instruments and dressings under Ben's direction.

This is fantastic. Is it really happening? she thought later as she watched Jude's skilled hands about their task, heard his calm questions to Ben and Ben's answers, and herself passed him the instruments which his gesture or a clipped word indicated.

The room, without windows, was virtually sealed and stuffy as no operating theatre ever was; flies buzzed in its shadowed corners and suicidal moths crashed the torch rigged overhead as an operating light. She had sterilized forceps, scalpels, clips – the lot – in water boiled in a *buchari*, the tea samovar to be found in every Eastern household, however poor, and instead of an aseptic cradle awaiting the birth, the two grandmothers were busy about swinging a little hammock, preparing a minute turban and passing a talismanic gold coin from hand to hand.

Yet here, as in real operating theatres all over the world and at the same moment of time, the exacting precision, the wonderful teamwork of surgery was going into action and achieving its confident purpose, step by unhurried step. For there wasn't, she reflected, any "miracle" to surgeons or their work. It was the dedicated skill of men like Jude Tarleton, like Ben Randall; it was their theatre nurses and all the technicians behind

28

them. It was the belief of everyone concerned that what they were doing was good and right and must succeed. It was –

But there coherent thought stopped for her. One moment her senses were fully alert and obeying her will; the next, wave on wave of imagined sound assailed her ears . . . receded . . . roared again, and it was as if every nerve she possessed were fighting a disabling battle against the mist of unconsciousness which threatened to engulf her.

Time escaped her. Later she could have believed that whole minutes passed, to be lost to her for ever. But in fact it was only a second or two before she heard Jude's voice, sharply corrective, speaking her name – "Martha!" and then, "Pull yourself together – you can't faint now" – and by an effort of will which hurt almost physically, she came round, seemingly without her hands having missed a movement which her brain had asked of them.

But she was swept by shame. Momentarily, as their hands touched in an exchange of instruments, Jude Tarleton's eyes met hers above their masks and she dropped her own. She glanced up to see Ben shaking a compassionate head at her, heard his muttered, "Take it easy. Won't be long now," and was grateful to him. But his sympathy did nothing for her chagrin, nor for her nagging suspicion that Ben's tolerance of her weakness was not shared by Jude.

After that, very soon it was over. There was the mewling, protesting cry she had heard a hundred times and more on maternity duty. There was a new life – a boy – to be cherished and loved and spoiled, and for the moment all the busyness of washing and dressing and cradling and, for themselves, of disrobing and clearing away their gear.

They left the tiny newcomer in his hammock under a gauze mosquito net. He was already wearing his turban and was swaddled from head to foot in cloth tied about with ribbon. He wore the gold coin on his chest and his chin and forehead were touched with a kohl beauty spot by one of his grandmothers, as a warding-off of evil and a protection from disease. The West had done its best for him and now the East was taking over.

Youssif helped to re-load the car. Ben was to stay until their patient came round from the anaesthetic. Youssif bowed out Jude and Martha with a gratified, "May Allah grant that the whole world love you", and a few minutes later they were on their way back to their quarters.

They were hearing them when Martha asked, "When and where do I ordinarily report for duty?"

Jude said, "At the hospital at eight, though you may have an hour's grace your first morning. Ben or I may pick you up when we're going at your time, but you shouldn't bank on transport, and Naomi can show you a short cut. Your mornings will mostly be in the clinic – casualty ward stuff – and you can usually reckon on being off duty during the siesta hours. But after that you'll collect some house visits to do after you've been here a little while, and you'll be on call to me or Ben except for your one day off a fortnight, which may be something of a movable feast until we've got some girls trained to help you, you understand?"

"Yes, of course. I didn't expect to be able to count on regular off-duty," she told him, and hurried on to the thing which had to be said before they parted. "I'm terribly sorry about nearly passing out on the job to-night – " she began, only to be cut short in mid-sentence.

"Forget it," he said brusquely. And then, turning to

look at her measuringly, "You certainly had a baptism of fire, and I've an idea you're going to do," he added, and could not have guessed how eagerly some need within her turned the guarded praise of that into a kind of accolade.

When she woke, too few hours later, her bedside clock made the time half past seven. There was silence from Naomi Troy's room and under Martha's door was a pencilled note from her housemate.

Naomi had written:

You were asleep when I left at seven a.m. to prepare some cultures for Ben in the lab. Saluma goes to the market at first light, but she will be back and can get your breakfast if you take it.

Always supposing Jude hasn't had the common humanity to give you the day off (and I wouldn't bet on it), here's how you can cut something off your trek to the hospital when you come over.

There followed a sketch map of the short cut Jude had mentioned, and then "Be seeing you", and the florid signature "Naomi T."

Martha bathed and dressed and, not wanting breakfast, had made tea for herself and was drinking it on the tiny verandah before Saluma returned, to be followed a few minutes later by Dorrit Randall.

Dorrit wore no make-up. Her nondescript straight hair was drawn into so tight a ponytail that its roots looked pained and her creased sailcloth shorts were too revealing of her plump thighs. The whole effect made her appear even younger and more immature than at her first meeting with Martha, who had difficulty in thinking of her as a married woman at all.

She flopped ungracefully into a chair and refused Martha's offer of tea.

"I had some with Ben. He came back from that case too late to make it worth while to go to bed and he's gone straight to the lab. I suppose *she*" – Dorrit's thumb seemed to indicate the absent Naomi – "has gone too by now, hasn't she?"

When Martha confirmed this Dorrit nodded glumly. "I hoped so. That's why I came over. Banking on Jude's having given you the day off, I mean – " Her voice trailed away as she intercepted Martha's quick glance at her watch. "You don't mean to say he *didn't*, after all you'd been through yesterday and his dragging you out on the case last night?" she demanded.

Martha said, "No. But he gave me an hour's grace. I haven't to be at the clinic until nine."

"Walking over?"

"Yes."

Dorrit jack-knifed more deeply into her chair, crossing her legs over its arm. "Not to worry. You don't have to. I'll take you in my car."

"Have you got a car of your own?" asked Martha.

"Uh-huh. My mother's wedding present to me. Or her thank-offering, more likely."

"Her thank-offering? What do you mean?"

"For being rid of me, of course, when Ben took me off her hands. She had never had any use for me, anyway –" Dorrit paused and met Martha's embarrassed glance truculently. "But you wouldn't know what that's like, would you?" she demanded. "You can do things. You've every reason to be confident and sure of yourself, and you can't ever have experienced what it is not to be *wanted* – "

"Believe me, I have," said Martha quietly.

"But not because you're as negative and feckless and

32

idle as I am," Dorrit countered. "You're probably talking about being turned down by some man. But everyone always wants to be rid of me as soon as possible. Or they radiate pity, which is worse. Like Ben. *He* only married me out of pity, and now I can *see* him regretting it and comparing me with slick women like Naomi and calm, capable ones like you. Take you, for instance – I bet when you wake every morning you know exactly what you're going to do with your day?"

"I suppose I do. Not exactly, but more or less, when I'm working," Martha allowed.

"Yes, well, I almost never do, for the simple reason that there's nothing I do well enough to care about making plans for it. I hate gardening and I'm a rotten cook. I tire of anything I do take up before I'm through. I'm just hopeless, and I know it, and Ben knows it too."

Martha said, "Nonsense. I should think a man almost never marries for pity alone, and if you worked as hard at doing something worthwhile as you have at convincing yourself you're a failure, you might be surprised at the result."

"But there's nothing worthwhile I want to *do*!" Dorrit wailed.

"I don't believe it. If there weren't, you wouldn't make such a thing of telling people you're a good-for-nothing. You'd be content to be one and leave it at that," was Martha's shrewd comment.

"You think so?" For the first time a hopeful doubt crept into the girl's voice.

"I'm sure of it." Martha drove home her point. "One could say you're more of an out-of-work than a born idler. There's a difference, you know." Pausing, Martha took a swift mental look at an idea which had struck her, then added, "Look, almost at once they're going to need more help in the hospital – especially to get a women's ward going. The idea is that I train some Bedouin girls as nursing aides, but what would you say to coming along too?"

Dorrit pulled a face. "Nursing? Oh, I couldn't! Sick people embarrass me, and I don't know the first thing about coping with them."

Martha said crisply, "You shouldn't flatter yourself you'd be nursing anyone for quite a time. But I suppose you could make a bed or use a duster or brew a hot drink, couldn't you?"

"Oh – sort of housemaid stuff?" Dorrit pursed her lips and shook her head. "Anyway, Jude wouldn't have me near his precious hospital. He hates me."

"Hates you? I don't believe it!"

"Despises me, then, and hates the idea of me. Anyone could see he was fit to be tied when Ben brought me back with him. And I know he thinks I come between Ben and his work and that I'm just a parasite."

"All the more reason then for proving you're nothing of the sort. So if I put up the idea to Jude, will you have a stab at it if he agrees?" Martha asked.

"He won't play," prophesied Dorrit. But Martha, herself convinced of the value of the plan, refused to share her doubts.

By day the one-storied building of the hospital looked stark and uninviting. At its far end a Nissen hut annexe was labelled in Arabic and English "Dispensary and Outpatients' Clinic", and when Martha made for its open door, she found Jude already there.

On benches round the walls his patients – all men – waited their turn, some gazing blankly before them, others comparing ailments with their neighbours. A

34

light twitter of voices and a child's whimper from behind a screen indicated that there were women patients too, and Jude, who was extracting grit from a young man's eye, told Martha he would join her in a minute and attend the women next.

Her appearance on the far side of the screen was the signal for stares from half a dozen pairs of dark eyes and some diffident giggling, and briefly she felt as panic-stricken as she had on the wards on her first day out of Prelim Training. But when Jude came to introduce her, there was a shy chorus of "*Salaam aleikum, o Tabiba*" which seemed to welcome and accept her.

With Jude came Ahmadi, his Arab assistant who had worked as a medical orderly in an Aden hospital and who interpreted Jude's diagnoses for Martha's benefit.

There was a septic hand for dressing, a bronchial cough, a toddler who had fingered the embers of a char-coal fire and a woman who produced for Jude a box of grubby white pills which he took from her and began to scold her roundly.

Ahmadi enlightened Martha. "They are malaria treatment tablets for which she asks money from *tabib* Tarleton."

"But how did she come by them?"

"From the *tabib* himself – who else?" chuckled Ahmadi. "He has prescribed them for her husband and she brings them back to him. It has happened before. Once it was a pair of crutches, another time a bottle of cod liver oil. But look – the *tabib* laughs as he sends her about her business, so that even that one, when she has a proper errand, will come to him again. For that is his way – first he is angry, but then he is gentle, and nobody who is sick need fear him for long."

35

After finishing with the women they returned to the treatment of the men, almost all of whom lingered afterwards in the courtyard, squatting on their heels in the glaring sun and gossiping over their bubbling hookahs.

One or two latecomers straggled in. Then Jude closed the clinic for the morning and showed Martha over the remainder of the building.

It comprised four main rooms – the men's ward where already a few bed-patients were installed, each attended by one or more of his relatives, the laboratory where Ben and Naomi were at work on the day's dispensing, another room, as yet empty, which Jude planned as the women's ward, and an operating theatre. Jude had a cupboard of an office opening off the laboratory, and there was a cloakroom for Naomi and Martha. The façade on the far side from the forecourt was less forbidding, with wide windows giving a distant view of the mountains and a near outlook on to a stone terrace set about with flowering shrubs in pots. It was so far from any European conception of a hospital that comparisons were impossible. But its very limitations were a challenge which Martha realized she was longing to take up.

There were people they had treated that morning who should have been admitted to hospital if they could be induced to come in and if there were staff to attend them. The sooner they had some help, however unskilled, the better. Meanwhile, there was the enlistment of Dorrit Randall to broach to Jude, and she did this on their way in his car to visit Youssif's wife and her baby.

He listened without comment, and when he spoke it was to ask a question.

"Do I take it Ben is a party to this scheme?"

Martha said, "Why, no. The idea only came to me while we were talking, and I promised I would put it up to you and see what you said."

36

"Then I'm afraid you're going to have to report back that the answer is no."

"*No?*" Martha echoed in disbelief. "But surely – ?"

"You heard what I said," Jude cut in. "No. That's final."

CHAPTER III

For a long moment Martha stared at his profile. "I don't believe you mean that," she said. "Or if you do, I can't think why."

"No?" he queried. "Well, though I could ask that you should accept my decision at its face value. I'll tell you why. I'm refusing to recruit Dorrit as a nursing aide for the simple reason that in my opinion she is a butterfly brain with very few aptitudes and less staying power, and your efforts to train her would be a pure waste of time. Fair enough?"

Martha shook her head. "No. Not as we are placed. We need help badly as soon as possible – "

"– And have an excellent source of it in view, as I've told you. The Bedouin girls I have in mind are biddable and will have nothing to unlearn. The whole of their time will be ours; there are more where they come from, and with little else open to them, we owe it to them to help them to make nursing their career."

"I see that. But between them and me, there'll be language difficulties for quite a time," Martha protested.

"Granted. But you have interpreters enough among the rest of us, and you'll best learn Arabic – as they will learn English – by the hard way of being forced to make yourselves understood."

"But Dorrit would be still another pair of hands," Martha protested.

"But for how long?" Jude countered. "For about the

time, if I'm any judge, she keeps the romantic illusion that nursing is a matter of soothing fevered brows in an attractive uniform which, in Taroued, it demonstrably isn't."

"Nor is it anywhere, and I've already warned Dorrit she would be coming in at first as a cross between a wardmaid and a teaboy, which is where most of us begin."

"And where the trainees I've engaged will expect to begin," he agreed evenly. "There's a posse of three sixteen-year-olds with seven years' schooling behind them coming up from Bab Magreb tomorrow. Until they can live in at the hospital they will be housed with a widow in the Quarter, and you'll find they have some English already."

Martha was silent. "Then I must tell Dorrit there's nothing doing?" she asked after a moment.

"I'm afraid so. Anyway, you had no right to give her any firm promise before you had consulted me," he reminded her.

She said stiffly, "I'm sorry, and I shouldn't have done if I had had any inkling at all that you would be" – her disappointment sought and found a strong word – "so obstructive about it."

Though his brows went up at that, he said nothing. She waited, and then, stung by his air of having settled the matter, she blurted, "Supposing your sister had lived to come out here with you, wouldn't you have been willing to let her choose, or have a say in choosing her own staff?" And then, regretting the graceless question as soon as she had uttered it, she added, "I – I'm sorry. I oughtn't to have put it like that – "

"But you did, and you make it quite clear that you think I'm being a monster of obstruction for obstruction's sake." He paused, then nodded. "All right," he said. "If Ben is agreeable to Dorrit's working, you shall play your hunch. You may rope her in on whatever terms suit you both."

Surprised by this unlooked-for surrender on his part, Martha said quietly, "Thank you. You're very – generous."

"But not in defeat. Don't think it," he retorted. "You haven't convinced me you can make anything useful of Dorrit Randall, and I'm simply bowing to the logic of your point that, since I'd have allowed Bonny her own mistakes, I shouldn't deny you yours. Passed to you and Dorrit now to prove me wrong and yourselves right."

"And supposing we don't . . . can't?"

"Then Dorrit will go out on her ear, and you'll be liable to get a kingsized 'I told you so' from me." But something in his tone softened the threat, and in return Martha felt a surge of loyalty towards him.

Loyalty to him, and for herself something akin to the sense of feeling backed by strength, secure, which she had known while she had believed herself sure of Greg Ryder's love.

If she needed a reward for her small victory, she found it in Ben Randall's gratitude. When he drove her back to her quarters at siesta time she edited him for her talk with Dorrit and asked him to pass on to her Jude's consent to the plan.

"Stout of you to tackle him," was Ben's comment. "And though my poor pet would go to the stake rather than admit it, regular work that's expected of her is just what she needs. Of course she could find it in looking after me and the house, if I had the heart to tie her down to mere domesticity when she hasn't a glimmer of a clue about it."

"She must have been very young when you married

40

her?" Martha prompted.

"Just eighteen. Her mother was a widow who was drifting from one chi-chi place to another in search of a second husband. But having Dorrit in tow didn't help the cause, and as she was always being reminded that she hadn't inherited any of her mother's looks or poise, she grew an inferiority complex about twice life-size. With the result that she now is convinced it's not worth her while to try her hand at anything, because she'll fail at it or lose interest for sure."

"I know," Martha nodded. "She said as much to me. She also claimed that Jude hated her, which I told her was absurd."

Ben confirmed, "So it is. Jude isn't the chap to waste anything as lethal as his hatred on anyone as adrift as Dorrit. But of course he makes no secret of his view that marriage and the conditions of this job don't jell, and Dorrit senses as well that he has no time for ditherers or people who don't pull their weight. As Naomi does. As Jude will expect you to. How do you think you and Naomi are going to make out as housemates, by the way?"

"Very well, I hope, though so far we've hardly met," Martha told him.

"Yes, well, I don't see why you shouldn't. After all, you don't have to take all that glamour and know-how of Naomi's as a personal affront in the way Dorrit does. You've got more than enough of your own. Meanwhile," Ben appealed as he opened the car door for Martha to alight, "you'll encourage Dorrit, won't you? Tell her she's doing well, even when she isn't, and try to make her go on, however much she says she wants to quit?"

"I'll do my best," Martha promised, thinking it as well not to emphasize that for quite a time Dorrit would only be exchanging one "domesticity" for another.

As she left him she was remembering a shade wistfully how, last night, she had thought of their small community as an easy-going but close-knit team which had welcomed her. Well, so it had. But within twenty-four hours it seemed to have contrived to draw her into its undertow of personal conflicts too. . . .

The next day the three Bedouin girls from Bab Magreb were flown up in one of the Company's planes. Jude interviewed them in Martha's presence, then despatched them by car to their lodgings, telling them to report for duty the next day.

To Martha's relief, they all spoke some English, and Mina, the eldest, who had been out from the school to daily service in an English family, was quite fluent. She was the most adult in her ways too. By contrast Jahra and Nura, who were sisters, were wide-eyed children. But whoever had short-listed them for the job had chosen well. All three could clean and wash and do simple cooking, and as early as their first few days on duty, Martha realized that they could be launched on the rudiments of nursing much sooner than she had expected.

Meanwhile Dorrit was reporting too, acting as Martha's driver to and from the hospital and sometimes on the after-care visits to patients which Martha increasingly made alone without Jude. Dorrit also sat in at the morning sessions in the clinic, tolerated if not approved by Jude and encouraged by Martha, to justify her presence in whatever way she could.

She proved to have more skills than she had claimed.

Her clerical work was neat and she was conscientious about the scrupulous cleanliness which Martha impressed on her. She asked intelligent questions and, best of all, she showed a talent not far short of genius in her dealings with children.

The gentle touch and the soft voice she used with them spoke a reassuring language which they understood. Their mothers might mistrust Jude's medicines and the babies themselves were loud in their resentment of his and Martha's ministrations. But scarcely a toddler who was brought to the clinic resisted Dorrit for long, and on that score alone Martha began to savour triumph.

But one morning, having waited in vain for the girl to call for her, she went alone to the other bungalow to find Dorrit still in dressing-gown and slippers. At sight of Martha she was on the defensive at once.

"Can you make it on foot this morning? I'm not coming," she said. And then, in answer to Martha's anxious question, "No, nothing is the matter. I'm quite all right. It's simply that I'm browned off with the whole idea, as I told you I should be."

"Oh, Dorrit!"

"Well, you can't say I didn't warn you. And what do I *do*? I wait around for you in the car, or I stand about in the clinic, listening to Jude speaking Arabic to the patients and watching you or Ahmadi binding them up or sticking them with injection needles or handing out drugs which everyone knows they only sell in the bazaar."

"But the tinies! Surely you've enjoyed helping with them?"

"When there are any, yes. They're sweet –"

"Well, you can hardly ask to have a supply of sick babies laid on, just so that you can justify the time you spend in the clinic," Martha retorted crisply. "Besides, you do a good deal more than stand about. While you're watching the rest of us, you're learning all the time. You and Mina and the others relieve us a lot of the practical chores, and you keep the patients' record cards,

43

don't you?"

"Yes, and get a rocket from Jude if I muff producing the right one on the dot!" said Dorrit with feeling.

"Well, Jude is a perfectionist, with a very good idea of the value of his time," said Martha, stating a truth she was learning herself by trial and error. "Anyway, you can't quit just like this, without any valid reason except that you haven't got the sticking power to see it through, or at least a bit further than you've gone."

"Oh, and why can't I?"

"Because, if you must know," said Martha, purposely brutal, "Jude prophesied that this was exactly what would happen. But when I said you ought to have the chance, he gave you the benefit of the doubt. So now I'm not making your excuses to him for you. You'll make them yourself. You owe him some kind of notice, so you can put in the morning at the clinic as usual and tell him afterwards if you must."

"I don't see why any notice is necessary. It's not like an ordinary job. I'm not being paid, and you can't say I asked for it, can you?"

Martha said firmly, "But I asked for it for you, so you owe something to me. I can't make you go in for duty, of course, but at least you could have the grace to drive me to the clinic, since I'm late already through waiting for you to collect me."

Dorrit appeared to waver. "I'm not dressed," she said.

"I'll give you five minutes – "

On the short drive Martha did not press the argument. She felt the chances of Dorrit's attending the morning's clinic were slim, and she was under no illusions that she had won any victory worth having when Dorrit alighted from the car with her and went in moody silence to don her overall. Ben's advice to wield the big stick had been a mistake, thought Martha. Dorrit's conviction of her shortcomings wasn't to be handled that way. But the right way completely escaped her, and only the kind of miracle which didn't happen was going to prove her judgement of the girl to be surer than Jude's. . . .

The morning's clinic produced its usual crop of minor to serious ailments. Jude attended the women patients first, gave some calcium injections for skin troubles, lanced a badly swollen "housemaid's knee" and was treating his last waiting patient to a brisk scolding for neglecting a burned hand when another woman sidled in, carrying a significant bundle in her arms.

Martha, who knew her for a young mother who had attended earlier with a five-year-old whom Dorrit had soothed to quietude when everyone else had failed, went over to her and touched the bundle gently.

"It is your baby who is sick, Khaera bint Hamid?" she asked in her rapidly improving Arabic.

Above the face-veil the woman's dark eyes met hers. "Yes, *tabiba*. The *tabib* — ?"

"A few minutes, and he will see you," Martha promised, and went to stand by when Jude signalled that he was ready. He clicked a vexed "Tch!" at sight of the stifling wrappings of the bundle, and as he drew them back from the baby's face, he looked sharply at the mother.

"Your baby is very ill indeed, Khaera bint Hamid. See, she can scarcely breathe, and yet you keep the good air from her! How long — ?"

Much of what the woman said in reply escaped Martha. But she could see for herself what was wrong with the baby. The purpling, suffused skin and roaring, tortured breathing told her experience their own story. This was diphtheria at the stage where the cruelly swollen throat tissues threatened to suffocate –

45

Jude was speaking again. "The child must stay here. If you will leave her in our care, we can help her to breathe and make her well again. But if you do not, she may die. Therefore she must stay."

The woman reached for the baby and took it back. "No!" she said.

"*Yes!*"

"No. I bring her here for you to cure her, as you cured my little Zora. But if you cannot – "

Jude said patiently, "Listen, Khaera bint Hamid. It was easy to cure your Zora – she had been eating too many dates. But it will take time to cure your baby, and if you take her home with you now, Zora may become ill too; or your husband may, or you yourself. The baby must be helped to breathe again, and quickly, and this we can arrange, I and the *tabib* Randall and the *tabiba*, if you will let us keep her here."

"You want – until tomorrow, perhaps?"

"No, longer than that. When she can breathe again, there will still be fever, and this we must watch while it lasts. But if you will allow me to prick your arm with my needle, you may come and be near her at night and watch her yourself while the rest of us sleep."

The woman hesitated. "And when I am not here? When I must care for my husband and my little Zora – who will watch the baby then?"

"All of us, but especially the *tabiba*."

"The *tabiba*?" The young mother's eyes went first to Martha, but then beyond her to where Dorrit stood in the background with the Bedouin girls. "That *tabiba* – the one who is so good and compassionate with my Zora and the other little ones – she will watch the baby?" she asked.

Momentarily Jude's face was a study. But his reaction was instant. Certainly his glance flicked in Martha's

46

direction, but at once he turned and looked back at Dorrit, then told the woman, "Yes, that one – the *tabiba* Randall – she shall be there."

"Then – " The gesture with which the baby was handed back was infinitely trustful. "I must go now? When am I to return?"

"At sundown, not before. The child will be better then. But first, Khaera bint Hamid, there must be my needle for you."

As he spoke Jude snapped a finger and thumb at Dorrit, and when she approached, looking her bewilderment, he asked, "Have you been immunized against diphtheria?"

"Yes."

"Then take a look at what's probably your first sight of a case," he said, and put the baby into her arms.

"*Oh!* How – " Her voice broke in pity, and then Martha was behind her, tying on a mask, and she cradled the baby in silence, watching as Martha prepared its mother's arm for the anti-diphtheretic serum and Jude administered it.

Afterwards matters moved swiftly. The waiting men patients were told "No clinic this morning" and departed with resigned "*Inshallah*'s – 'Allah wills it"; Ben was sent for, the theatre was prepared and the delicate, relief-giving work of tracheotomy was ready to be done.

Dorrit had nursed the baby until it had to be prepared for the operation, and when Jude was scrubbing up he called her to him.

"Well, how does it feel to be the instrument of getting us our very first female in-patient?" he asked her.

Her puzzled glance went from him to Martha, waiting to help him into his gown. "Wh – what do you mean?"

47

"Just that. Don't you realize that it was my promise to Khaera bint Hamid that you would be taking a turn with the after-care of all this which tipped the scales in our favour?"

"Why, no! I – That is, I didn't know what she was saying, what was going on. She wanted *me*? Not Martha? Me? But why?"

Martha, watching them both, found Jude's smile very good to see. He said to Dorrit, "Just one of those things. Seems you've got what it takes for the mothers of babies to love you and believe they can trust you. So what do you say? Will you come on to a more or less round-the-clock rota of duty with Martha and the others?"

Dorrit's eyes shone. "*Will* I?" she asked rhetorically.

"Good. Martha shall organize it as soon as we've got the job over."

"Over? What are you going to do?"

"Nothing very terrible. Open the windpipe and insert a tube, so that air passes through that while the child can't breathe in the ordinary way," Jude told her. "If you think you can take it, stand by and watch. If you can't, better make yourself scarce until we've finished."

Dorrit stood by. Martha guessed she was needing all her moral courage to do so, but she did not flinch, and afterwards she waylaid Martha.

"You hadn't told Jude?" she asked.

Martha, her mind preoccupied, echoed blankly, "Told Jude? Oh, you mean about your wanting to give up? No."

"Then he needn't know, need he? I mean – now I don't want to tell him. Because if it's true that the baby's mother really asked for me, it makes all the difference, makes the whole thing a lot more worth while somehow. You see," Dorrit added awkwardly, "except

48

when Ben asked me to marry him, I can't remember anyone's really *wanting* me, singling me out, choosing *me* before, and I sort of want to – to keep faith – d'you know?"

Martha smiled. "I know. That's how feeling needed does take one, I think – grateful for the chance and set-teeth determined to be worth it." She was thinking, but did not say so aloud, that it seemed some miracles did happen after all.

The word went swiftly round the Bedouin quarter. Khaera bint Hamid had left her sick girl-child, night and day, at the hospital, and no harm had come to it. By Allah's will it was cured and returned to Khaera. And now, it was said, there were others who feared less than they did to put themselves into the *tabib's* and *tabibas'* care –

So, slowly but inevitably, the hospital's list of in-patients grew. The women's ward, primitive as to staffing and equipment as it was, became a continuing reality, and a month after Khaera bint Hamid's baby was discharged, Martha delivered her first Bedouin baby in the maternity annexe to it.

In those days it seemed to her that she worked all the hours there were – in the clinic, on house and tent visits, on the wards and in the practical tutoring of her aides. Everyone else worked as hard, she knew. But the de-manding routine and the savage heat took the greater toll of her, and she envied Naomi the buoyant resilience which took her out evening after evening on her return from the laboratory.

True, Taroued's resources of relaxation were strictly limited. But Naomi went the rounds of the impromptu parties in the oil personnel's quarters, and whenever she was free, rarely lost the chance to jump any plane which

49

happened to be flying down to Bab Magreb.

She was impatient of Martha's off-duty lethargy and her disinclination for parties, of necessity almost wholly all-male and which tended to go on too long.

"You're simply playing Jude's game and letting him get away with it," Naomi accused.

Martha, just back for an hour's siesta and with another tour of duty before her, flopped into a long rattan chair and allowed her back to know the sheer luxury of its support. "Get away with what?" she asked.

Naomi, lacquer brush at the ready, surveyed the fingernail she was about to paint. "Why, this pretence of his that all of us up here, hes and shes alike, are wrapped in separate little cocoons labelled 'Devotion to the job' and since that's the way he wants it, that's the way it is."

"I thought the 'No wives, no fiancées' rule was the Company's," commented Martha.

"Nominally it is. But if Jude said the word that a little mixed society wouldn't be such a bad thing, d'you suppose the Company wouldn't come into line? No, it's Jude's own gimmick for keeping us all nose-down, and if he's so blind as to deceive himself that it works – for him, any more than for the rest of us – that's just too bad, and his rude awakening is something I don't mean to miss."

Martha caught at a phrase. "What do you mean – Jude deceives himself that it works for him?"

Naomi shrugged. "Oh, up here it has to, if only for the sake of the example. But he goes down to Bab Magreb, doesn't he? And to Aden – no?"

"Yes, but – " Martha felt herself flushing, and Naomi laughed.

"I see you get the idea," she said. "What's the betting our respected Chief makes a beeline for the bright lights for the same basic reason as the other men do – for relaxation? Anyway, thanks be, I'm due for a week's leave in Aden myself on Saturday, and I hear he is flying down on the same plane. So to prove my point, tell you what: If I suggest he takes me out to dinner that night and he agrees, I'll see that we both have a good time. But if he refuses, we'll know he probably has a lot more dubious fish to fry. Want to be there when I ask him?"

Martha rose, collected her scattered belongings and trailed tiredly towards her room. "I don't see that you'll know anything of the sort," she said. "For instance, had you thought that if he wants you to dine with him, he might prefer to ask you himself? Or be dining with friends? Or have some professional business to do?"

Naomi ignored the first two suggestions, fastened on the third. "My dear girl, be your age, will you?" she drawled. "We don't touch down until sunset, and who, I ask you, does business in a city like Aden after dark?"

As it happened, though Martha was present when Naomi put her suggestion to Jude, she was not within earshot of his reply. But across the room Naomi's cynical smile and turned-down thumb were significant. Evidently Jude had excused himself, and Naomi was inviting her to share conclusions which she found hateful without knowing why. Later, by a Box and Cox chance which her hours of duty sometimes caused, they did not meet again before Naomi left for Aden, and Jude had gone too.

The next morning Martha woke to a Sunday which, saving an emergency, was all hers to use as she liked.

Since Sunday had not the same meaning for the Bedouins as for the Europeans, there would be a clinic session as usual. But Ben would deputize for Jude; Dorrit and Ahmadi were helping him and two of the Bedouin girls would be responsible for the light evening duties on the wards until Martha herself went back for night duty, with Ahmadi also sleeping on the hospital premises.

While the morning was still cool she worked a little in the garden, grubbing at the soil of a narrow strip beneath the bungalow windows where a few zinnias and sedalcea struggled for existence. As she worked she thought how badly gardens needed loving planning over years, and how poor were this one's chances if the Company failed to strike oil within the next few months.

The desert would encroach on it, snatch it back. Neither it nor its neighbours would outlive the first few dust storms, the cruel winds. And the fate of abandoned gardens, empty houses, would be the least of the tragedy. The hospital too . . . all it stood for. Jude's work. Jude's future. And where would she herself be a year hence? she wondered.

She had run away from England, from the pain of still loving Greg. If she had to, could she face running back again? Or, in her secret heart, did she perhaps crave an excuse to go back; to hear news of him, which shouldn't be difficult, in order to test how far she had grown away from him or whether she had escaped at all?

In her waking hours she could tell herself she had been wise. But sleeping, there were still the occasional dreams of him which, unasked, made him still the dearest reality of her life and tore cruelly at her conscious will to forget him.

When the noon sun became intolerable she took refuge beneath the extended sunblind of the living room window, ate her lunch there and settled to write some long-overdue letters home.

She began one to Grace Armour; wrote copiously for a time; slowed up and only realized she was drowsing, cheek on hand, when her pen dropped with a clatter on to the table.

She gave up then and lay back, drifting off again almost at once, dreamless until it happened. . . . Until Greg was there, nebulous, dim of outline, but holding out his hand to her, only to turn away and laugh when she put out her own to grasp it.

She had the illusion of taking him by the shoulders, trying to turn him about. That was part of the dream. But her despairing, "No, Greg – no!" was spoken aloud and woke her to the realization that her face was wet with tears and that she was no longer alone.

CHAPTER IV

Jude stood there watching her, his expression unreadable for the moment before he turned away. To her desolate, confused mind the movement was strangely inseparable from Greg's dreamed rejection of her. Momentarily she was as much hurt by one indifference as by the other. But Jude's gave her the chance to knuckle away the welling tears and to steady her voice to say, "I didn't know you were there. I'd fallen asleep and had a horrible dream – "

He turned to face her. "So I gathered," he said, and paused. "Do you want to talk about it? Work it out of your system? It sometimes helps."

She shook her head. "No . . . it's fading. It wasn't very clear."

"As you like." He was looking up at the canvas of the sunblind. "That's not enough protection at this time of day. If you're going to sleep at siesta time you should lie down on your bed under your net."

She indicated the sheets of her letter to Grace. "I was supposed to be writing letters. I slept late this morning and I didn't mean to drop off." Controlled now, she added, "I thought you would still be in Aden. When did you get back?"

"We touched down half an hour ago. I'd done what I went for and I meant to come back today. And when Sellars, who was piloting, mentioned that the padre from Bab Magreb was due up this morning for his monthly visit to Base, it occurred to me that you might care for me to drive you over for Evensong at four."

"I'd like that very much."

"Then get whatever approximates to your bonnet and we'll be on our way. I'll wait for you in the car."

Base, some miles east of Taroued, was an encampment of maintenance workshops, store sheds and hangars, grouped about the airstrip. A large mess hall had been adapted as a temporary chapel, and when Jude and Martha arrived, about a hundred men had assembled for the service. The sweet, familiar words of the prayers, the unaccompanied hymns and the short sermon which went straight to the heart of the problems of exiled men, all did much for Martha's depression after her dream, and when they came out she thanked Jude warmly for bringing her.

"I hoped you might enjoy it," he said. "I always do. Seems we're not the only ones either. Once the word goes round the outcamps that it's Padre Dobson's Sunday, nothing short of a find of oil which couldn't be checked would keep the men away. Come and meet the Padre, and then" – he looked at his watch – "when are you due on duty?"

"At ten. Dorrit will drive me and I planned to sleep for a couple of hours first."

"Well, I'll get you back in time. But if you haven't yet explored any of the Tarjol, we might drive up through the Wadi Ghali as far as the road goes. The view up there is worth seeing, and while you're here we mustn't cheat you of such scenery as there is."

To reach the long valley through the foothills they skirted Taroued and began to climb by way of a twisting stony road where the only signs of life were the lean hares which were startled by the car and the partridges no bigger than song-thrushes which pecked avidly at the sparse vegetation of the verges.

For some miles Jude concentrated on the road and the remarks they exchanged were punctuated by long silences. Then he said, "Tell me, how much gossip have you heard about our chances of survival, supposing Murray and his team don't find before the Company's concession runs out?"

Surprised by the question, Martha said, "Some. Why?" In fact, talk came round to the subject all too frequently for her liking.

"Because," Jude said, "I want you to scotch any you hear in future and refrain from passing it on. Our chances are still fifty-fifty – either Murray will strike oil or he won't, and until zero hour we've got to think success, for the simple reason that we daren't think failure."

"Daren't?" Martha echoed.

"Too strong, you think?" He shook his head. "It isn't, believe me. Let a breath get round the markets of the Quarter that we aren't here for good, that we are only using our patients as guinea-pigs before moving on, and while their trust of us is still on a razor's edge, we can say goodbye to the lot of them overnight. And not only to the patients, but to any staff – orderlies and so on – we may need to recruit. Do you see?"

"Yes, of course."

"Good. Meanwhile," Jude went on, "we can't blink the fact that if Murray can't show results, both the Base and the hospital's future will be at the mercy of Sheikh Seiyid Alim. So last night, with Murray's blessing, I bearded the gentleman on the subject."

"Last night?"

"Yes. I'd asked an audience of him at his Aden town house. That's what took me down there – What's the matter?" he broke off as Martha audibly caught her breath.

56

(Impossible to explain, even to herself, that stab of relief that Naomi's hints as to his errand had been wrong.) "Nothing," she told him. "What did the Sheikh say?"

"A great deal in his most suave vein. He invited me to dine with him and to stay the night in his private apartments. But he intended I should get the message that he wasn't in the concession-granting business for his health, and it's anyone's guess as to whether or not I made my point about the hospital's dependence on his renewing when the time comes."

"But if he cares for his people at all, surely he must appreciate what you are trying to do for them and what it would mean if the hospital had to close down when the Company moves out, if it has to?" Martha protested.

Jude spread a hand. "You'd think so. And if he doesn't understand the position, then my Arabic isn't as dynamic as I thought it. But he'll stall all the same. The East, as you probably know from your father, doesn't have much use for the straight answer."

"Does the Sheikh live all the time in Aden?"

"No, he has another house in Bab Magreb."

"I meant, does he ever travel round his Sheikhdom? Does he ever come to Taroued?"

"He hasn't been in my time, though he tells me that as a young man he hunted ibex through every valley for miles around. Why, are you thinking he could do worse than come to see for himself what we're doing?"

"Well, wouldn't it be a good thing if he did?"

"It would indeed. I'd had the same idea myself – of getting the Company to invite him to inspect Base and of laying on a kind of Open Day at the hospital for him. He would probably come if we spread ourselves on ceremonial and unrolled enough red carpet. Yes, I'll put it up to Murray and Dumont and we'll talk it out. Meanwhile – " Jude nodded ahead, "this is the end of our road. Beyond this it's only mule-tracks. But if you like to get out and look back and down, you'll get a good view of Taroued and the way we've come."

They alighted and went to stand on a jutting shelf from which it was possible on one side for the eye to follow the ribboning road almost all the way down to Taroued, nestling in the shelter of the lower slopes. At that distance it looked frail and vulnerable, a mere shanty town at the pitiless mercy of the desert.

On the other side of the shelf the terrain stepped far down by jagged levels to a heat-misted emptiness which might have been anything. Clouds below an aircraft had the same baffling, shrouding quality, thought Martha as she watched Jude adjusting and using binoculars on the mist to no purpose.

"Believe it or not," he said, pointing, "there's a level of moor-cum-marsh down there."

"Marsh? I didn't realize these regions knew the meaning of the word!"

"Where else do you suppose we breed our finer malaria mosquitoes?" he retorted. "No, the curiosity is that the Bele upland – that area – should be so high and still pocket so much stagnant moisture. I was hoping to get a sight of it from up here through the glasses to see whether the summer rains have done anything to flood it out. But I doubt if they've been heavy enough this year."

As he spoke he was putting away the binoculars, slinging the case around on to his back. " 'Know your enemy'," he quoted. "I'm going down. If I'm right and the place is a hotbed of stagnant pools, the oil boys must get cracking on it as soon as may be."

"What can they do?"

"Well, though they haven't found oil for themselves yet, they have gear for spraying crude oil on the surface of still water; the mosquito larvae come up to breathe, the breathing pores fill with oil and – *finis* for that brood." He paused and looked about him. "You're not afraid to be left with the view for company until I get back?"

"Of course not."

She watched him go, a tanned, muscular figure in the uniform of every European in Taroued – shorts, open-necked shirt and rope-soled sandals. Once she thought he looked up and straight at her and she waved to him. But he climbed on down unheeding until the mist swallowed him. Then she crossed the shelf for another look at Taroued and afterwards set out to explore the track which climbed easily to the next level, from which she could look directly down to the parked car and out and down on her left to one of the last sights she would have expected.

Flowers. Tall cosmos, golden-rod, moon daisies – they grew in terraced profusion as if their seeds had fought a winning battle with cactus and thorn for every inch of fertile soil pocketed between one harsh rock and the next.

Hungry, these many weeks, for such colour and lush growth, Martha stared, calculating the hazards of climbing down and gathering an armful before Jude returned.

From where she stood the ground fell away in a steep drop. But though there was no path in sight, there were scrubby plants for a handhold and boulders to act as a brace for the feet. She began to step down crabwise, testing each sideways step before giving her weight to that foot. Once some loose scree betrayed her and she had to let herself go, half running, half slithering into the lee of a waist-high boulder.

She leaned against it, getting her breath before rounding it. On that last scurry into its shelter she had caught at a cactus plant or two and, aware of an odd sensation in her palms and fingers, she glanced at them to see a crop of minute hairs adhering to them. Nothing to worry about. They were only hairs, not thorns. Scrubbing her hands on her skirt, she left her boulder and a minute later she was plucking at the resistant stalks of the flowers.

She was less heeding of her balance as she gathered, cradling her spoils in the crook of one arm. She had enough now. She must go back. She straightened, felt the quick throb of vertigo from stooping – and saw the yawning fissure that had been hidden by the flowers' foliage a split second too late to save herself from it.

She swayed, arms windmilling, flowers scattering. Then her false step where nothing was took her down ... down, six feet, eight feet and more until she touched bottom where the fissure V-ed inward. Down there she had scarcely room to turn; one wall of her prison faced her, the other was at her back, and the level from which she had fallen was a good foot beyond the uttermost stretch of her arms.

Shocked and frightened, she waited for a few minutes. Then she tried to knee and claw her way upward. But her fingernails only rasped fruitlessly and she had to abandon the attempt. Her hands too, from prickling hotly, had begun to turn painful, and she thought they were swelling. She rubbed them together and again on her skirt for comfort, and wished with all her heart that it hadn't to be Jude who would be forced to search for her and rescue her from a folly she need not have blundered into.

How long had he meant to be away? He hadn't said. When he did not find her by the car, he would look for her and shout, no doubt. But would her answer carry to him? She tried a tentative call, but the thin mountain air only carried it away, and there was nothing for it then but to wait and strain her ears for Jude's coming.

She heard him at last, calling her name, sharply, worriedly, from the track, and then he was above her, treading the undergrowth through which she had crashed, and kneeling at the edge of the rift, looking down at her.

"Martha – what the devil? Are you hurt?"

"No, only a bit shaken. It was the flowers. I wanted them, and I never saw this until I stepped into it," she said lamely.

"Stepped into it! Famous last words – you might have broken your back. These slopes are riddled with this kind of fault, and when I left you I credited you with more sense than to start shinning down the nearest rock face alone."

"I told you – I wanted the flowers." Shock was having its way with her, and to her chagrin she heard her voice quiver on the edge of nervous tears.

Jude said, "Tcha – !" and then was scuffling into a prone position, reaching over the edge to her. "Give me your hands and knee your way as far as you can, to give me enough purchase to haul you up," he ordered.

But his iron grip on her swollen hands was too much to bear, and after a second or two of exquisite agony she had to wrench free and fall back.

"I – can't do it. My hands – "

He knelt back on his heels. "Take a rest and we'll try again," he advised.

She shook her head. "I still couldn't, I'm afraid. I don't know what's happened, but my hands feel as if they'd been scraped raw."

"Then we'd better try a rope. I've got one in the car."

Sooner than she hoped he was back, making a loop in the rope, passing it down to her and belaying the other end round a boulder.

"Sit in the loop and hold on above the knot," he

ordered. "I'll haul until you're level with the edge, and if you can manage to hang on for a second and take the weight off the rope, I'll help you over."

She "hung on" by digging her elbows into the edge when she came level with it. Then, his hands on her waist, he was helping her to scramble to her feet and, still holding her, watched her closely as she straightened and found her balance.

"All right?"

Her mouth lifted wryly. "Yes. I suppose it *was* pretty idiotic of me, wasn't it?"

"It was," he agreed dryly. "Don't try conclusions with the Tarjol again until you're mountaineer enough to test every step before you make it. But now for these hands of yours. What's wrong with them?"

As he spoke he took them both in his, turned them palm upward and uttered a smothered exclamation. He jerked his head at the nearest cactus. "I suppose you used some of those things for a handhold as you came down? And scrubbed hard at your hands as soon as they began to smart?"

"Yes, but I hadn't pricked them – only collected a lot of tiny hairs. *Those*," she nodded at a few which still adhered to her fingertips.

"Exactly. But 'those' happen to be the trouble; from that particular species, they're poisonous. Sit down, will you? I'm going to have to pull out as many as you haven't successfully rubbed beneath the surface of your skin, and down below you'll have to have a shot of penicillin to localize the septicaemia set up by the rest."

When she sat he knelt and with meticulous gentle care worked over every inch of her hands from fingertips to wrists. His touch was as coolly clinical as was his murmured "Sorry" when now and again she winced, and there was nothing . . . nothing at all, Martha told herself, which could explain or excuse the sudden racing of her pulses at his nearness.

It was only memory, of course. It *had* to be only memory of how, alone with Greg and as close to him, it would have needed no more than a light endearment from either of them to take them into each other's arms. For there wasn't any parallel. Jude was as emotionally unaware of her as of any other patient, and it was sheer heady madness of her thoughts to use the same wavelength for him as they had done for Greg. A secret madness that didn't show. But madness, for all that; as unreal as a mirage and about as empty of reward.

Satisfied at last that he had done all he could for her hands, Jude helped her to her feet and guided their way back to the track and the car. She was touched and grateful when, on the way, he stopped to gather more flowers for her; she had delayed their return enough already, she told him, adding, "I shan't manage much more than a catnap before I go on duty."

"On duty – with your hands in that state?" He shook his head. "On the contrary, you're getting your penicillin as soon as we get back, and then you're going off to bed for eight hours straight," he told her.

"But I must!" she protested. "Dorrit has been on the clinic today. Jahra and Nura must go off, and Mina can't be on duty alone – "

"She needn't go on at all. I'll sleep at the hospital myself." His tone allowed for no argument, and a minute or two later he changed the subject by asking, "By the way, I suppose you've been waiting to hear me eat my own words in the matter of young Dorrit? All right – seems you were a better judge of her than I was. Will that do?"

Martha smiled. "It would, handsomely, if I had been right and you had been wrong."

"Well, wasn't I?"

"Not altogether. At first Dorrit didn't want you to know this, but I doubt if she could care less, now that she's so keen," said Martha, and went on to remind him of the incident which had caused Dorrit's change of heart.

"Well, it seems to have had a lasting effect. But if all she needed was to feel wanted, I'd have thought Ben's four-square devotion would have done that for her," was Jude's comment.

"You'd think so," Martha agreed. "But I gather she had managed to persuade herself he could only have married her out of pity."

"Pity? A healthy young animal like Ben? Nonsense. Why, one wonders, must women distrust any motives that aren't spelled out for them, letter by letter? For instance, a job like Taroued and romance don't mix. Besides being my view, it's an unwritten law of the Company's. But when Ben wanted to marry Dorrit, he rode roughshod over both, and if that doesn't say anything to her about his strength of purpose, it should. What's more, instead of doubting Ben, she could employ her time better by proving the lot of us wrong."

"Ah, but would you – or the Company – admit it if she could?" Martha countered.

"Why not? As long as Ben shows he can keep his eye on the ball while he's on the job, he and Dorrit can go as cosily domestic as they please."

"But not the rest of the men? Not . . . you?"

"The rest of the men are the Company's business, and you may be sure it knows what it's about when it rules they stay single for the term of their contract. As for myself" – Jude paused and shrugged – "I'll cross the bridge of a clash between Taroued and marriage when I come to it."

"And if you have to lose this Taroued, there will be others for you?"

His chin jutted. "That is the kind of subversive talk I've warned you against. I've told you, I'm not interested in the possibility of losing this one until I've actually lost it. But if I must – yes, almost certainly there'll be others for me."

It was an answer which seemed to take him miles away already, and into a time and a world she would not know.

The penicillin did its work on her hands and she took duty again twenty-four hours later, none the worse for the experience. The bungalow, free of Naomi's mercurial presence, was a more restful place. But she returned the following Saturday, as glossily poised as ever, with a week of riding, swimming and golf, and night-long Aden parties behind her.

Over their first meal together she mused to Martha, "I wonder how our respected Chief spent his weekend in the Big City after all? I'd give a lot to know which particular *boîte* he favours. But naturally he's not telling."

To that, not without satisfaction, Martha said, "He spent his one evening in Aden dining with the Sheikh, and more of the next day than he bargained for winkling *me* out of a chasm on the Tarjol."

Naomi's brows arched. "Good heavens! How come?"

When Martha told her how, she commented, "Jude *must* have been pleased with you! What sized rocket did you collect?"

"No bigger than I deserved. In fact, not much of a rocket at all, considering the nuisance I'd made of myself. And he actually gathered some more flowers for me before he brought me home," said Martha.

"Well, I must say Jude picking buttercups and daisies for anyone is a sight I hate to have missed," Naomi drawled. "But by the same token, as he has never taken *me* tête-à-tête up the Tarjol, I suppose I should now ask myself what S.A. have you got that I haven't?"

Martha said dryly, "I don't think you need bother." And knew from Naomi's short laugh that she agreed she needn't.

That was Naomi, relaxed, urbane, coolly friendly. There was another Naomi, crisp, shrewd and efficient, in the laboratory. And yet another, far less likeable, as Martha was to realize before the next week was out.

Naomi broke the storm by coming to the clinic one morning after Jude had gone on his rounds and Martha was directing Mina's clearing up. Naomi was set-faced as Martha had never yet seen her, and she lost no time in voicing the accusations she had come to make.

"Look," she began with a false air of tolerance, "I can appreciate that, just because Jude asked you out for a pleasant Sunday hour, you may think you're the kingpin with him. But all the same, what do you mean by running to him with this story of my refusing you the use of the lab for your nursing pep talks to the aides?"

Martha drew herself up. "I have *not* run to Jude with any such story!" she denied.

"Then who has? How does he know anything about it?"

"I haven't an idea, unless Ben told him," Martha offered.

"Ben didn't – "

"Then I wouldn't know. Dorrit, perhaps. But anyway, let's get it straight. I know you made some difficulties about our using the lab for lectures, because Ben told me as much. But as it rests with Ben – or with Jude – to give us permission, you haven't the say-so either way, have you?" Martha pointed out.

Naomi snapped, "Apparently not, if Ben gave you

the green light without consulting me. But that hasn't stopped Dorrit or whoever making trouble for me with Jude. He came to the lab last night, flaming at all four corners, and tried to tell me exactly where I got off."

"Well, I'm sorry," said Martha. "If it was Dorrit, and it must have been, I'll have a word with her, or ask Ben to."

"Which is going to help the point at issue a lot, I must say! How do you suggest Ben and I are supposed to run a research lab with you and your hordes of adolescents swarming round us?"

"With Dorrit, three aides and four boy orderlies and rarely all at once," Martha commented evenly. "Naturally too, we shouldn't be there when you or Ben are carrying out path. work. But there isn't anywhere else where I can show the necessary charts and diagrams, and it was Ben's idea that it would also do them a lot of good to see what a few million germs look like under the microscope."

Naomi sneered, "I daresay they'll be all eager eyes, and not least for any handy drugs they think they can flog in the market!"

"What nonsense! Every one of them is trustworthy; they'll never be alone in the lab, and surely neither you nor Ben leave drugs lying about?"

"We still have to use them, and up till now we haven't had to worry about the odd cupboard door left unlocked for a minute or two. However" – Naomi turned on her heel – "if any do go missing it'll be your headache. And you can tell Dorrit from me that I'll accept her apology any time she likes."

But Dorrit remained unrepentant, claiming that at Naomi's persuasion Ben had begun to have second thoughts against the scheme.

"And if that didn't justify my getting Jude to O.K.

it, what did?" she wanted to know.

So, though Martha's tutoring went ahead in the laboratory, it made for almost as strained relations between herself and Naomi as already existed between Naomi and Dorrit. Mainly through Dorrit's fault, Martha had to admit. For something about Naomi seemed to bring out the worst in the younger girl, and not least was Dorrit infuriated by Naomi's aloof contempt for the hostility Dorrit could not hide. A hostility which, a week or two after their latest clash, took her to the point of an accusation for which she had no shred of evidence and which, when Martha appeared on the scene in mid-skirmish, Naomi was demolishing with obvious enjoyment.

"Must I repeat that I couldn't be bothered to hatch an affair with Ben?" she was asking.

"And if you aren't, why are you going back to the lab five nights out of seven lately? Or *are* you both at the lab all the time, I wonder?" Dorrit accused wildly.

Naomi watched one of her cigarette's smoke-rings widen and dissolve. "Why don't you ask Ben?" she suggested.

Martha took a hand. "Don't bait her," she admonished Naomi. And of Dorrit she asked, "Why pretend Ben hasn't told you Jude thinks he has tracked down the local source of the bilharzia epidemic that took hold in the Quarter during the summer, and that he asked Ben to go all out with the research on it?"

Dorrit admitted sulkily, "Well, of course I know that's what takes Ben back to the lab. But why does *she* go along too?"

"Maybe," offered Naomi, falsely sweet, "it's because I'm funny that way and I get a kick from holding hands with Ben by the frail light of a Bunsen burner. It couldn't of course be because Ben needs me there when he's on research, could it?"

"All right," Dorrit allowed. "But where do you go on afterwards? Trust *you* not to finish off on evening without getting in on some party somewhere! Last night, for instance, Ben came home just around midnight, and I suppose you were both in the lab peering at snail sections or something until then?"

"But last night," put in Martha, "Naomi wasn't out, and I happen to know Jude and Ben had their heads down, discussing the arrangements for the Sheikh's visit. Ben must have told you that too, Dorrit."

"I didn't see him before he went out. And when he was so late back, we had a row and I wasn't going to ask him. But that was only one night – " Dorrit rounded again on Naomi. "Of course I know Ben isn't really interested in you, except that he thinks you're a good scientist and that you've got all sorts of know-how I haven't. But you'd like to line him up along with all the other available men you manage to collect, wouldn't you? What's more, I wouldn't put it past you to imagine you could have Jude dangling too! Yes, even Jude. Why don't you try training your sights on him as well?"

Naomi affected gratitude for the suggestion.

"Thanks, pal. It's an idea. Perhaps I may, at that," she said, her glance sliding to Martha and back again to Dorrit's incensed face. "Perhaps I may."

"Well, do let me wish you luck," Dorrit jeered.

"And what," posed Naomi unanswerably, "makes you think I need luck to get any man I want? Even – I'm quoting you, dear! – the monastic Jude!"

CHAPTER V

Sheikh Seiyid Alim had chosen to make his ceremonial visit to Taroued by road from Bab Magreb, rather than by air from Aden. The Desert Patrol was to escort his retinue as far as the guard post, where Jude and Ben and the chief seismologist would meet it, leaving soon after sunrise in order to do so. The Sheikh was to inspect the hospital first, then the base camp, and be driven out to watch some of the nearest soundings. That night he would sleep in a luxury version of the traditional Bedouin tent, sent ahead and erected for the purpose, and had invited the oil chiefs and the hospital personnel to dine with him there.

Martha, who had taken night duty the previous night, had asked Dorrit to clock in especially early, so that all the essential ward work could be finished before the great man arrived, and everything was well in hand when Dorrit came to say that the Bedouin girls' landlady wanted to see Martha.

"She asked for Jude first, and for you when I told her neither he nor Ben were here. I don't know what's the matter, but she's all of a dither, wringing her hands and muttering, and she's been crying, I think," said Dorrit.

"Crying? For goodness' sake, there's nothing wrong with any of the girls, is there?" worried Martha.

"There can't be, with either Mina or Jahra. They came with the old girl and they're getting into uniform now. Come to think of it though," Dorrit pondered, "they were both looking rather pipped, and Nura hasn't shown up."

"She wasn't supposed to. She did all-day duty yesterday and she's off until noon." Martha put aside what she was doing and rose. "But I'd better see Kalifa Fatma, I suppose, though I only hope my Arabic is equal to understanding what it's all about."

She was to find that Dorrit had not exaggerated the woman's distress. She refused to sit at Martha's invitation and stood with bent head, ceaselessly wringing her hands and only whimpering in reply to Martha's tentative questions.

Martha tried asking whether Nura had been taken ill, whether Kalifa Fatma herself was ill, what other trouble she might have at home – all without result at first. But Martha persevered, and gradually the story emerged.

Nura had run away, without telling even her sister where she was going or why. She had slept in her bed, but must have slipped from the room the three girls shared while Kalifa Fatma had gone to the communal well to fetch water. That had been at first light, and Nura had not returned since.

"But what makes you think she has run away?" asked Martha. "Why should she not have gone to the market to buy something, or to a friend's house?"

Kalifa Fatma shook her head. Her charges knew they must not visit the market alone, and already she, Mina and Jahra had, between them, inquired for Nura of all their neighbours.

"And if she has run away from you, you do not know why she should do such a thing?" pressed Martha. "Had you scolded her for something, perhaps?"

But no, she had not been scolded. Nura was a good girl. They were all good girls. There was no reason for her flight, the woman claimed, except that last night

71

Nura had been unhappy.

"Unhappy? How do you know?"

"She weeps. She does not tell what her sorrow is. But she weeps, and this morning she is gone. *Inshallah*."

Baffled, Martha sent Dorrit for Mina and Jahra. But though questioning them was easier going, both denied that Nura had confided in them.

"But last night she was afraid," offered Jahra shyly.

"Afraid? Of what? Of whom?" asked Martha.

"I do not know, *tabiba*."

"And before we slept she asked me how far away were the Outer Tents, and I told her I did not know," said Mina.

"The Outer Tents?" Martha and Dorrit, knowing them for the furthest outlying Bedouin encampment, some twenty-five miles west of Taroued, looked their perplexity at each other, and it was Jahra who proffered a clue to her sister's question.

"We have a relation, an uncle, who lives in the Outer Tents, *tabiba*."

"Then if Nura was really unhappy or afraid, it's possible –"

"– that she may be trying to get out to this uncle, you think?" put in Dorrit as Martha broke off.

"Well, don't you? From her having asked Mina how far it was?"

"But how would she go?"

"She would have to walk. There's no other way."

"*Walk?* Twenty-five miles? Under that sun? She'd never make it!"

"I know." The picture of the child's lonely figure, trudging doggedly towards a goal she might never reach before she collapsed from heat exhaustion, was one from which Martha shrank. She glanced at her watch, calculating times, then said to Dorrit, "Look, on the off-chance that that's where she has gone, I'm going after her, if you'll drive me."

"Now?" Dorrit looked at her own watch. "But there isn't time! The Sheikh – "

"I've thought of that. But I can't see that I've any choice. There's just a chance that if Nura hasn't got very far we might get back in time. If not, we've got to pray that the Sheikh's party won't arrive on schedule."

"Right." Dorrit nodded doubtful agreement and went out to the car while Martha, after explaining their mission to Kalifa Fatma, sent her home and collected flasks of water and some food for Nura from the hospital stores.

She and Dorrit briefly debated whether they should first tour the market booths. But there a European car always attracted too much well-meant attention, and even if Nura were there, it was fairly hopeless to find her in the milling mass of humanity which crowded the market at that hour. Instead they took to the road, discussing as they went what panic of fear or trouble could have taken the girl in such headlong flight. But nothing emerged. Once Dorrit said, "You know, this could be the wild-goose chase of all time. She might be *anywhere* – even trying to head back to Bab Magreb."

But to that Martha said, "I doubt it. Even she must have realized she hadn't a hope of getting there. No, lacking any other pointer, I'm sure we were right to follow up the hint about her uncle."

After that they were silent, straining their eyes ahead and neither caring to voice their deeper misgivings for Nura. Now and again on the outskirts of the town they had stopped to ask if anything had been seen of her. But nothing had, and now it seemed they were the only travellers along the narrow scree track which served as the road to the Outer Tents.

Already they had gone much further than they had

73

calculated they might have to, and both realized how precious time was escaping them. But suddenly, just as Martha was about to admit that their quest was hopeless and they must abandon it, she spotted Nura, crouched at the track side in the meagre shade of a thorn bush, her head dropped almost to her knees and one hand limply clasping the rough stick she must have cut to help her on her way.

As the car approached and slowed, she looked up, shading her eyes, then scrambled to her feet and began to run. Within yards they caught up with her, and Martha was out of the car, taking her by the shoulders and turning her gently about.

"Nura! Where were you going? Why did you run away?"

At their work none of the girls wore native dress, but for some reason Nura had reverted to it for her flight, and above the skimpy face-veil her eyes were dark with the terror of a small animal at bay. She stirred her shoulders beneath Martha's firm hold, but she did not reply until Martha had repeated her question.

Then she said, "I must run from the *tabiba* who is angry. If I stay, terrible things will happen to me. She said so. Therefore I go – "

"The *tabiba*? Which one, Nura?"

"The *tabiba* Troy."

"*Naomi?*" Martha exchanged a puzzled glance with Dorrit, then asked Nura, "Why was *Tabiba* Troy angry with you?"

"She says I take rich things from the room where she and *Tabib* Randall work. I do not see rich things and I do not take them. But she says yes, and that she will make much trouble for me with *Tabib* Tarleton. So I go," the child repeated.

"When was this?"

74

"Today."

"Today? Oh!" Martha had remembered the Arab custom of counting each day's date from sunset to sunset. "It must have been last night," she explained in an aside to Dorrit, and the rest of Nura's story confirmed this.

Painfully, punctuated by gulping sobs, it came out.

The previous evening, before going off duty, Nura had gone as usual to return the drug basket to the laboratory. Ordinarily she would leave it outside the locked door, but finding this open she had taken the basket inside and was leaving when Naomi had come in to accuse her of loitering and of having taken something valuable – Nura was not clear what – from one of the work benches.

Nura asserted she had begged Naomi to search her, in proof that she was concealing nothing. But Naomi had contented herself with the threat that she would hear more of the matter, and had then dismissed her. And as she had thought no one would believe her innocent in face of Naomi's word against her, she had decided during the night to run for sanctuary to the only blood relation, except Jahra, whom she had.

Her pathetic story told, at first she resisted all the girls' persuasion that she would not be in trouble if she went back with them. Knowing they must not appear as her gaolers, they agreed they ought not to force her, and though by now time meant everything to them, they merely pointed out that in resting in the car while she ate and drank, she was committing herself to nothing. But at last Nura was prepared to allow that she owed it to Jahra and kind, worried Kalifa Fatma to go back, and they were able to set out on their belated return journey.

"Naomi!" spat Dorrit. "How on earth did she hope to make an accusation like that stick? And what was she claiming Nura had stolen?"

75

"I don't know. Drugs, I suppose. And I've an idea," said Martha slowly, "that it was as much a move against you and me as it was against Nura."

"You mean because of that fuss about your using the lab for tutoring?"

"Yes. It didn't help when you wouldn't apologize for appealing to Jude about it, and Naomi probably saw this as a way to prove her point to him."

"You're suggesting she may have deliberately laid a trap for Nura by going out and leaving the door ajar?"

"I'd hate to think so. No, I only meant she saw her chance of pointing the obvious moral when she found Nura in the lab alone."

Dorrit laughed shortly. "Hah! I wonder –?" As she saw Martha glance yet again at her watch she broke off to ask, "I suppose you left a message for Jude, saying where we had gone?"

Martha nodded. "Mina knew, and I told her to tell Naomi as soon as she arrived, if she wasn't in the lab already."

"And are we going to make it?"

"Not a hope now, I'm afraid. Certainly not in time for the Sheikh's arrival. We're over an hour behind the deadline I'd set for our getting back, and as his tour of the hospital was due to take an hour, we're going to be lucky if we're even there for the end of it."

"Which Jude isn't going to like a little tiny bit," said Dorrit.

In order to avoid the delay of dropping Nura at her landlady's house, they took her on to the hospital. But that their luck had not held was only too evident when Ahmadi came out to meet them in the forecourt and to confirm that the Sheikh's party accompanied by both doctors had left for the base camp a quarter of an hour earlier. And *Tabib* Tarleton had shown himself very

76

ill pleased over *Tabiba* Shore's absence, Ahmadi volunteered.

"But he heard where we had gone and why? Miss Troy would have told him?" Martha queried.

It appeared, however, that only Jude's displeasure had registered with Ahmadi, and Naomi, when Martha went in search of her, did nothing to allay her misgivings.

Naomi said coolly, "How could I tell Jude any more than I gathered from Mina – that you and Dorrit had chosen to go off on some harebrained search for Nura, just because she hadn't turned up for duty?"

"*Not* because she hadn't reported," Martha corrected. "Because she had run away in the small hours, too frightened and distressed even to confide in Jahra. And I should think you, of all people, should have been able to tell Jude what had made her as desperate as that."

Naomi's brows lifted. "I? Are you suggesting she took herself off, just because I'd read the Riot Act when I found her nosing round the lab last night?"

"You did more than scold her. You accused that poor scared child of stealing from the lab, though she hasn't a clue as to what she was supposed to have taken, and she even offered to let you search her, in proof that she was innocent!"

"Which I was to deduce from the gabble of Arabic to which she treated me, I suppose? And isn't that exactly what you'd expect her to say, if she had been lifting stuff?"

"*If* she had!" Martha pounced on the phrase. "You mean you knew she hadn't taken anything when you accused her?"

Naomi urged impatiently, "Oh, be your age. Of course I didn't know then. The kid was there; I thought an unbroken box of a thousand sulphonamides had been on the bench when I'd left the lab a while earlier. So

I accused her – who wouldn't? It wasn't until later that I found Ben must have put the things into the drug cupboard before he left."

"And you realized your mistake – when?"

"Last night."

"And did nothing to put it right with Nura?"

"What could I do? She had gone off duty by then. And how was I to know she was going to run berserk like that?"

"You must have known how badly you had frightened her. But I daresay you meant to."

"At the time I did indeed. What's more, I didn't consider it would hurt her to stew until this morning, when the whole thing could be cleared up."

"And though telling Jude this might have gone a long way to make him understand why Dorrit and I hared off as we did, you didn't tell him any of it?"

Naomi shrugged. "When he asked where you were, I certainly didn't buttonhole him and reel it all off in front of His Sheikh-ship. I simply told him what I had heard from Mina and they carried on with the inspection of the clinic and the wards without you. But if it will help, I'll see Jude and Confess All before he has you on the carpet about it."

Martha said coldly, "Thanks, even if it is a bit late now."

"You're welcome," said Naomi airily. "And to judge by our respected Chief's expression when he found one of his senior staff gone A.W.O.L. today of all days, the case for the defence is likely to need all the boost it can get."

Before the inevitable interview with Jude Martha had no illusions that it would be an easy one. But she was unprepared for the sharpness of his condemnation of her

78

reaction to the morning's crisis.

Yes, he said, Naomi had now admitted her part in the affair. But though she should have been more guarded in her accusation of Nura, he was accepting that she had sincerely believed at the time that she had caught a thief redhanded.

"Naomi tells me she came on duty this morning with every intention of making amends for her mistake. So that lets her out. And now," he invited coldly, "since you knew the particular importance of your being on hand today, perhaps you can explain why you dropped everything and went off yourself on this rescue operation of Nura?"

Martha said, "I'm sorry. I suppose it must look very irresponsible to you. But at the time it seemed the only thing to do, and I did it."

"Merely on the thread of the question you say Nura asked of Mina about the Outer Tents?"

"It was the only clue we had as to where she might have gone, and someone had to act on it," she pointed out.

"But why you – in the headlong way you did? Why not have sent Dorrit with an orderly or have radioed Base for a search jeep to go out?"

"Because I didn't know whether they would send one; if there had been any argument it meant more delay where Nura was concerned. Besides, if we found her, I thought I was probably the best person to persuade her to come back. Dorrit hasn't enough Arabic, and Nura almost certainly wouldn't have listened to one of the boys."

"And I suppose you would plead that when you set out you thought you could do all this in the time you had before we were due with the Sheikh's party?"

Martha hesitated. Then, resolved that not for a second time would she bid for his approval at the price of her honesty, she said, "I – hoped we could. But – "

"But what?"

"Just that I ought to tell you that, however little time I had had, I'm fairly sure I should still have acted as I did."

"Even though you knew the importance I set on your being here when the Sheikh came at my invitation? On our being able to show him the hospital in action with a full muster of staff on duty?" Jude demanded.

She raised troubled eyes to his. "If it meant saving Nura an hour's distress or bewilderment she needn't suffer – yes."

"I see." He studied her for a long moment. "And you don't regard that as a pretty odd interpretation of your duty to me? To act on a single impulse of ill-informed pity and let any long-term consequences to the hospital go hang?"

"It wasn't a spur-of-the-moment impulse. I admit I was acting on guesswork. But I knew what I was doing, and it *was* my duty, I thought."

As their glances held, again there was a space of silence. Then Jude commented dryly, "Well, thanks at least for your candour, even if you're not to be congratulated on either your timing or on your idea of which are top priorities and which aren't." He paused. "Where is Nura now?"

"She's here. We brought her back with us. But I took the liberty of sending an orderly to tell her landlady she's safe."

"Then send her to me, will you?"

Martha supposed he meant that as his dismissal of herself, but she checked as she turned to go.

"Yes, what is it?" he invited.

"Nothing," she told him, and went on her way.

For though her impulse had been to beg him to be gentle with Nura, she had seen in time how little he merited her doubt that he would be. After all, it wasn't Nura who had failed him in loyalty or duty, and to the weak, the fearful or the defenceless Martha had never known him other than kind.

If the day had treated her better, she knew she would have looked forward more to the unusual evening in prospect. But she had not seen Jude again, and though Ben had been all sympathy, that was not the same thing at all. Later Jude and he had returned to the base camp together; Naomi left with one of the oil executives while Martha was showering and changing after coming off duty, and when Dorrit came for her Martha was doing her best to whip up her enthusiasm for an occasion she would as willingly have missed.

As they set out the sun was sinking towards the Tarjol and, as always happened towards that hour, the harrying, nagging wind of the season had dropped to the merest lazy fanning of the spiralling smoke from the evening cooking fires. It was the hour when the market booths were closed, the men went to the mosque for the sunset prayer ritual and the women gathered at the roadside wells to draw water into earthenware and goatskin and to bandy the gossip of the day.

On the road to the base camp there was only one semipermanent Bedouin encampment, served by a well a quarter of a mile distant from it. Here the movement was as colourful and noisy as usual; children ran and shouted in games of tag among their mothers' skirts and the women's laughter and talk echoed on the still air. But suddenly, when Dorrit had driven past by fifty yards or so, there rose a different sound – a stampeding of many feet which caused both girls to look back in alarm, and as Dorrit hastily put into reverse, a long agonized keening which chilled the blood.

They drew level and were out of the car, running, as a woman broke clear of the crowd, stumbling under the dead weight of the burden across her arms. Nearer, they saw she was carrying a boy of about eight, his head lolling lifelessly and his thin clothing dripping with water. Then the crowd closed in round her again, and the girls had to push through it to where the child now lay on the ground.

He did not appear to be breathing, and the froth of fluid about his blue lips were grim evidence to the tale everyone but his stricken mother was clamouring to everyone else.

"The little one plays. He runs, he trips; he falls forward into the well's mouth. The water is high and there are hands to draw him out. But it is too late. Already he is dead. *Inshallah*."

But Martha, dropped to her knees beside him, could feel a light flutter at his pulse. She looked up at the mother. "Your child is not dead," she told her. "We can help him, but you must help him too. You must send one of your friends back to your tent for dry clothing and warm coverings for him."

"It shall be done, *tabiba*." An older woman at the mother's shoulder spoke for her.

"Quickly, then!"

As Martha spoke she turned the boy over, noting as she made a pillow of his bent arms for his head that he appeared to have suffered no injuries. Then she was bending to the rhythm of artificial respiration and watching for the first signs that it was having results.

For too long – for what seemed an age to her straining muscles – it had none. Dorrit, watching anxiously, offered to take over. But Dorrit's knowledge of first-aid techniques was still elementary, and though Martha was damp with sweat and her back and arms ached intolerably, she carried on until the foul water began to trickle from the child's mouth and his reluctant lungs drew an independent breath . . . then another . . . and another.

"He is alive. He breathes. Allah be praised!" said everyone to everyone, and the grateful mother paid Martha the rare respect of a kiss upon her shoulder. Then the warmly swaddled boy was loaded into the car, and at the direction of many eager hands, Dorrit drove to the roadside tent which was his home.

On the way he was emphatically sick, but when Martha had superintended his putting to bed with a cup of warm goat's milk and a wheaten cake, he seemed none the worse for his experience. Martha promised the mother that one of the doctors should see him the next day, and both girls went out once more to the car.

"Well – !" began Dorrit on a long-drawn breath. And then, "Martha, honey, your dress! Just look at it, will you? *What* are you going to do about that?"

Martha looked, though knowing only too well what she would see.

Where she had caught the skirt of her white dress on a nail which had protruded from the main tent pole a triangular tear flapped open; there was a crescent tide-mark at the hem, and it was painfully evident that when young Abu Ben had thrown up, she had been within range. She leaned against the car door and ran her fingers through the damp tangle of her hair, as she fought her need, born of strain, to laugh and cry at the same time.

"Just . . . just not my day!" she tittered weakly. "How d'you do, Miss Shore – have you met any influential Sheikhs lately? Ne'er a one, sir; ne'er a one! Oh yes, I had the chance – two, in fact. Then why didn't I? Because both times I was too late on the draw – "

Fortunately Dorrit knew how to deal with rising hysteria. As Martha broke off, she pulled her upright and shook her smartly.

"Martha, be serious!" she urged. "We'll have to go back and let you change, and Jude will just *have* to understand what made us late this time!"

But Martha, herself again, shook her head. "No, we're too late already. It would be better for you to leave me here and go on. If you don't, Ben will be getting anxious, and I daresay he'll be able to arrange for one of the camp jeeps to come out and take me home."

"All right, though I hate leaving you," Dorrit agreed reluctantly.

"I'll go and sit with Abu Ben while I'm waiting."

"But you aren't just going home? You'll change, and make whoever comes for you wait and bring you back?"

"I don't know. Ask Ben whether it will be worth my coming back." Martha watched the car disappear into the deepening dusk, but did not keep her promise to return to the tent. It had been so hot there and she needed air. Instead she found a handy boulder at the roadside and sat on it, clasping her knees and watching the stars prick the sky one by one. The brightest of them, whose first visibility a month earlier should have marked *suhail*, the season of lessened heat, this year had done nothing of the kind. The days were still torrid and the nights little cooler than when she had come to Taroued nearly four months ago.

From a long way off the lights of the approaching car raked the darkness, and she was on her feet, waving it down, before she saw that it was Jude's, with Jude himself at the wheel.

He had scarcely braked before he was out, reaching for both her hands. "Martha, my dear! Thanks be! Are you all right now?" he urged.

As surprised by the small endearment as she was

touched by the disquiet in his tone, she said a little shakily, "All right? Of course – why shouldn't I be?"

"Because Dorrit said she suspected you were all in, but that you had insisted on her leaving you. Come here –"

Gently he propelled her into the path of the car's headlights, his eyes measuring her bedraggled appearance as his touch went to her wrist in search of her pulse. "Meanwhile, how's the boy?" he asked.

"Quite recovered, I think. Asleep, one hopes, if he hasn't been smothered by all the mother and aunty love he was collecting when we left," Martha smiled.

"I'll have a look at him." Jude took his medical bag from the car and opened the door for her. "Get in, will you, and when I'm through we'll be on our way. Are you going to feel equal to changing and coming back, do you think, or would you rather call it a night and go to bed?"

"I'd like to come back if you think it's worth it."

"It's worth it," he said. "Which tent?"

When he returned he drove fast for Taroued and came in to wait for her when she told him she could change and be ready again within a quarter of an hour.

But it seemed that once again she had reckoned without her personal gremlin. In her room she stripped quickly, re-did her face and her hair and had stepped into a pale green halter-necked dress when the zipper of its long back-fastening caught and stuck an inch or so above the waist. Frantically, remembering too late that when the same thing had happened once before Naomi had had to come to her rescue, she picked at and struggled with the tab, indifferent as to whether she forced it up or down as long as some movement on its part served to free her.

But the minutes ticked by and it still resisted all her efforts. She split a fingernail on it, and her arms were

85

aching almost as much as they had done earlier in a more worthy cause when she heard Jude cross the hall from the living room and knew he was listening for sounds of movement from her.

There was nothing for it. Holding the draped front of the dress up to her bare shoulders, she opened the door to him and told him diffidently what had happened.

"Well, time is going on. Why didn't you call for help?" he wanted to know.

"I – " She flushed with embarrassment. "I thought I could manage and that it must shift one way or the other any minute."

"Well, let's have a look. Turn around, will you? No, not that way. To the light – "

As he stooped to the recalcitrant tab, mastered it after a second and drew it smoothly to the top of the deep V of the bodice, neither his manner nor his touch could have been more matter-of-fact. "There," he said to her back. "Simple." But then, to her face as she turned to thank him, his tone rough and insistent, he asked, "When you found you couldn't cope, why on earth didn't you call me? What were you afraid of, Martha?"

She stared at him, meeting in his eyes something of the hard accusation they had held for her that morning. "Afraid of?" she echoed. "Why, nothing. I told you, I thought I could – "

He cut in, "All right. My mistake – you weren't afraid. So skip it. It doesn't matter."

But as she picked up her bag and he stood aside for her to go ahead of him out of the room, she wondered what he would have said if she had answered his question with the truth.

That she *had* been afraid. Not of any amorous opportunism on his part, but of herself. Afraid of experiencing again, at the intimate touch of his hands, the same secret longing as she had known on the Tarjol; of wanting to turn into his arms as, in reward of the small service, she would have turned into Greg's. Afraid of the enduring need of her heart and her body to love and to show it, even though there was no longer a Greg to show it to, nor anyone else to whom it mattered any more than it now did to him. . . .

Four hours later, after an evening unique in Martha's experience, Ben was an additional passenger in Dorrit's car for the return trip to Taroued.

The Sheikh, holding court under the blue-and-gold-starred panoply of his rank, had received Martha graciously on Jude's smooth introduction of her as the hospital's nurse-in-chief who had been "unavoidably absent" at the time of the official visit, but who had since – within the last hour, in fact – been privileged to save the life of a boy-child who was of the Sheikh's people.

Later, at the ceremonial dinner, the Sheikh had directed that she should sit at his right hand, and was lavish with his congratulations whenever she managed to reply to his questions in Arabic without needing Jude to interpret for her.

The meal had been spread, Arab fashion, at a level low enough for the guests, seated on cushions and leather pouffes, to help themselves with ease.

There were roast cuts of mutton served on piles of saffron-tinted rice, minute chickens fried in oil and innumerable dishes of salad vegetables and peppers in highly spiced sour cream. The dessert pastries were brightly coloured and as cloying as the coffee was bitter. When the dishes of each course were in place there was neither waiter service nor table cutlery provided. The solid food had to be conveyed from communal dish to plate and mouth by way of the right hand, and the sauces were drunk from individual bowls.

Afterwards there were sword dances by a troupe of male dancers to the beat of feet and drums, and an aged conjurer who, among other amazing tricks, broke pieces from a sugar cone, threw them aloft and conjured baby chicks from them before they reached the floor.

Beyond the open-sided tent facing outward to the desert nothing stirred in the black velvet night, and when the Sheikh's retirement to his private quarters indicated that the festivities were at an end, Martha felt that the switch from the East of the tent's dim interior to the West of the base camp's garish neons had the impact of a cold douche.

The Europeans had gathered in the camp bar for a while before separating to the various cars. On the way back Martha asked Ben whether the Sheikh had given Jude any firm promise as to the future of the hospital, only to be told no; that Jude hadn't looked for any direct result so soon.

"One day, out of the blue, the gentleman may come down in a big way on our side," said Ben. "But as, naturally, he would prefer the Company to foot the bill, Jude thinks he may postpone his offer – always supposing he'll make one – until almost the zero count-down of the concession. Meanwhile, what did you make of this evening's Arabian Nights entertainment?"

"It was fabulous, something quite out of this world," said Martha. "I had to keep reminding myself I was really seeing it all and hearing it and living it – "

"Not to mention eating it?" chuckled Ben. "When we get in, I'm going to prescribe a soda bic. mixture for Dorrit and myself. Like a dose too, just in case?"

Martha laughed. "I doubt if I'll need one. I didn't over-eat, if only because I found feeding from my fingers rather off-putting, and because I avoided the more unrecognizable things."

Ben agreed, "I know. I'd begun to think rather wistfully about an honest joint and two veg myself. However, when you get back to England, think of the line you can shoot about having dined with a Sheikh, even if they aren't the romantic dreamboats they used to be! Which reminds me," he added as Dorrit pulled up outside Martha's quarters, "when Jude went back to pick you up, did he backpedal at all on the rocket he gave you this morning over Nura?"

"No, he didn't mention it. Why?" asked Martha.

"Only that he insisted on going back for you himself. Which gave me to wonder whether Dorrit's story of how you had coped with young Abu Ben had clothed him in sackcloth and ashes and he wanted to make amends. Otherwise, why not send me or one of the oil bods for you – ? Hullo–ullo?" Ben broke off to nod at the darkened bungalow. "Naomi not back yet? Will you be all right?"

"Perfectly," said Martha. "I hardly thought she would be in yet. Gil Brancaster took her over, you know – "

"– but isn't bringing her back," put in Dorrit. "Before we left Base, I heard her ditching Gil like mad. And for – "

"Don't tell us, let us guess – for the Sheikh in person?" suggested Ben facetiously.

"Joke – funny ha-ha!" his wife withered him. "No, believe it or not, for Jude. '*Oh, Gil, even if Jude has been a bit attentive lately, I hadn't an idea he was expecting to take me home tonight. But you do see it's just one of those things, and that I can't very well refuse? Now, Gil dear, don't be like that – there'll be other times. See you –*' " Ah well," Dorrit dropped her sour mimicry of Naomi to add, "I suppose you could say I dared her to it. Remember, Martha, how she boasted she could get even Jude in tow, and I said 'Better go

89

try'? Well, now evidently she is trying. What a hope!"

"And *you'd* better watch it, puss-puss," chided Ben mildly. "For let's face it, Naomi is quite a gal for those that like the type, and even the Judes of this world must *have* a type, wouldn't you say?"

"Not Jude. Where girls are concerned, he's barely human, and if he is bringing Naomi home, it's because she has asked *him*, not the other way about. I mean, Jude suddenly going all masterful he-man and coveting Naomi enough to filch her from under Gil Brancaster's nose – it's just not possible! Well, *is* it?" Dorrit appealed to Martha.

"I don't know," said Martha, realizing as she said goodnight to them both and got out of the car that she wanted to believe in the possibility as little as Dorrit did.

CHAPTER VI

At last the intense heat was gone. Now the days had the clear quality of a St. Luke's summer, and at sunset the temperature dropped sharply.

Sleeping was easier and so was working. Accident treatments at the clinic were as numerous as ever – camels were still ungallant enough to bite, and carelessly guarded fires still burned unwary limbs – but there were far fewer cases of summer sickness among the babies and of malaria and dysentery for the wards.

Personal tensions eased somewhat too. Immediately after her clash with Naomi over Nura, Martha doubted their ability to maintain even the "live and let live" front which, by tacit consent, they had set up before it. But Dorrit's suggestion that Martha should move into the spare room of the Randalls' bungalow had been promptly scotched by Jude.

Martha, he ruled crisply, would stay where she was. On Dorrit's own showing, she was no housewife; she and Ben ate only when she was moved to cook, and it was no part of Martha's duty to be saddled with the kind of chores which Dorrit could neglect if she pleased, but which Saluma should continue to handle for Martha.

At first the downright veto on her change of quarters had irked Martha. But she appreciated the reasoning of it. She had a job to do, and Jude was right, it wasn't housekeeping for three. So she settled for the inevitable; she and Naomi continued as housemates, talking shop over meals and, for politeness' sake, each mentioning plans which affected the other, but never exchanging confidences nor touching any sympathetic chord at all.

It was a cold-blooded relationship which was quite foreign to Martha's warm nature. But at least it kept the peace, and Naomi seemed quite unaware that anything was missing from it. In fact, Martha doubted whether she had ever enjoyed a friendship with her own sex. Naomi was a man's woman to her core and liked it that way.

With the generally slackened pressure of work Martha now had more free time and was looking forward one morning to spending the afternoon cutting out a new dress for Dorrit when Mina came from the lab with the message that Jude wanted to see her there.

In the lab he was at the card index of blood-groupings which had been compiled from among the patients, the hospital staff and the men of the oil community, and one card – Martha's own, she noticed – lay on the table beside the index drawer.

He nodded to her, finished flicking through the drawer, then closed it and picked up her card.

"Look, Martha," he said, "as our only AB negative, you've got a job on. I take it you've donated blood before?"

"Yes, regularly, in England," she told him.

"But not on emergency call?"

"No. It's such a rare group that I don't think Meerstead ever put out a call for it while I was there."

"Well, we've got an urgent one now – by radio from Bab Magreb. The hospital there has an AB negative patient with multiple injuries after a car smash. They've radioed Mukalla and canvassed the Aden blood bank, so far without result. So if you're willing, I propose to send you down as soon as Base can lay on a plane to take you. You'll go?"

"Yes, of course. Shall I get back tonight?"

Jude fingered his chin thoughtfully. "You'd better take a change and overnight things, in case not. I know one aircraft is in dock, so if Base can't spare the other to wait for you, you may have to stay over. Anyway, the hospital will give you a room, and I'll arrange to have you fetched by air or road tomorrow."

An hour later Martha was aboard the plane, flying south above the road she had not travelled since her arrival in Taroued. With no cargo but herself and the pilot aboard, the flight was bumpy, and she was not sorry when she first sighted the sea and the town beneath the wing and felt the plane lose height for its landing.

David Sellars, the pilot, saw her into the car which had been sent for her from the hospital. He himself, as Jude had thought possible, had to return at once to Taroued, but he would be back to collect her tomorrow, he promised.

At the hospital there was better news of the patient she had come to serve. Aden, after all, was to supply two other samples of compatible blood, and with the pint Martha would give, there was good hope of saving him, she was told.

Afterwards she was shown to the small balconied room which had been provided for her, and when she had showered and freshened up, it was with a sense of stolen holiday that she went out for a look at the town.

Dazzlingly white, it nestled at the foot of its cliffs, facing across the gentle curve of its bay towards the evening sun which gave it its name – Bab Magreb, Sunset Gate. It had no distinction of "quarter" – except for a few officials and the hospital personnel its European population was negligible, and it was almost wholly Eastern in character – flat-roofed and narrow-streeted

93

and doing its age-old trading in cloth and food and brass-ware from wall-booths, and bargaining for spices and carpets at the harbour when the great dhows, plying between East Africa and the Persian Gulf, stood off in the bay.

Martha spent a tranquil hour sitting on the harbour wall, watching the fishing boats dance on the bright sea, and debating with herself just how many fish each fisherman had managed to crowd on to the arms of his shoulder-yoke before setting off to sell his catch in the evening market. But when the early dusk began to fall and the air chilled, depression suddenly came down on her like a cloud. She felt lonely, alien, marked by too many strange eyes, and knew – as she had never done yet in Taroued – that she would give anything for an escort on her devious, shadowed way back to the hospital.

Arrived there, it was good to be back in her own world, to talk shop at dinner with the Scots surgeon on her left and to try to make her scant German understood by the Austrian doctor on her right. Afterwards she went to bed early, slept until she was called and was packing, preparatory to going out to the airport to await her transport back to Taroued, when a radio message was brought to her.

There was no plane available to fetch her today. The one in which she had come down had developed engine trouble and was in dock along with its fellow aircraft. But Jude was bringing a patient down to the hospital by road and would take Martha back with him on his own return. Meanwhile she was to stand by and wait until he arrived.

When he did, it was already late afternoon. She was sitting in the shade of a giant cedar in the hospital garden when he came to tell her his patient was a man from Base with an impacted wisdom tooth for extraction, who would have to be warded for the night, in order for him to recover completely from his "general".

"That means you and I will be staying over too, and the three of us going back in the morning," said Jude. He sat down on the sparse grass beside her chair. "How did things go for you yesterday? No ill effects, I hope?" he asked.

"None. They let me see my donee this morning, and he's doing fine too," she told him.

"Good." He leaned for support on his hands outspread behind him and looked up at her. "Then if you're agreeable, I suggest we give ourselves an evening on the town. For instance, as I drove along the coast road I noticed that a couple of dhows were in, which means, at this time of year, that their cargo will be carpets. How would you like the chance to buy yourself a Persian rug?"

"Very much," said Martha. "But I couldn't afford one, I'm afraid."

"I don't know. You could be surprised by the price. Haggling is expected of you, and it all depends on your staying power. Anyway, there'll be nothing doing until after siesta. But we'll drive down to the harbour before dark and try our luck, and afterwards we'll dine in the town and do whatever it has to offer. Will you be ready in, say, an hour?"

Martha said she would be ready whenever he was, and when she went to her room to change she wondered where her last night's malaise had gone. For today her mood was relaxed and carefree, and at the thought of the evening in Jude's company she experienced the lift of spirits which children know at the promise of a treat ahead. Some inner sense told her that it would prove a time she would remember when other things and times of her year east of Aden were blurred and ultimately forgotten.

In the bay the two dhows, their sails struck, rode remote and aloof from the feverish activity their arrival had caused on the quays, where seamen were unloading bale after bale from their dinghies and unrolling a fortune in carpets at the feet of the interested crowd.

The bargaining began. Prices were mentioned, rejected as absurd by the customers, new ones made. Carpets were returned to the dinghies in high dudgeon, brought out again and re-offered at a new figure. Darkness fell; everyone, carpets included, repaired to the Customs shed, where the business continued by the light of lanterns and naphtha flares. It was all great fun and, despite the vendors' despairing cries and gesticulations, extremely goodnatured.

Jude bid on her behalf for a small blue and yellow rug and on his own for a larger wine-red and blue one. More than once both transactions broke down completely. But Jude advised her not to worry. If they returned to his car, it was more than likely both rugs would soon be there too. Which, indeed, they were, and Martha's at least at a ridiculous price which she could well afford.

Jude drove to the gardens surrounding the principal square where, he said, was the town's only restaurant worthy of the name. There were *boîtes* and night-haunts they could visit later to see some Eastern dancing, but they would dine best here at *Fanus Hussn*, The Lantern House, where he was known.

He chose a table on the patio which was lit by candles and by the fairy lanterns looped into the trees. Above them the tops of the trees were a dark silhouette against the sky; then that too was quite dark and trees, sky and everything beyond the lighted patio were mysteriously one.

As they sipped their aperitifs Martha said naïvely, "You know, last night for some reason, suddenly this town scared me. Yet tonight it seems quite different – friendly again and asking to be liked."

Jude set down his glass. "Last night? I hope you weren't trying to cast round it on your own?" he asked sharply.

"No, but I went exploring it during the afternoon – "

"You said last night," he reminded her.

"At dusk, then. On my way back to the hospital I was jumping at every shadow and felt I was making myself conspicuous by being out at all. Which was doubly silly really, because I never feel like that in Taroued, and Naomi says that, if she has to, she goes about here alone without any embarrassment."

Jude said shortly, "Well, if you come down alone again, don't try it. In Taroued you've no reason to fear unwelcome overtures; you've earned people's respect there and everyone either knows you or knows of you. And Naomi's freedoms are no comparison either – she was born in Aden, she is cosmopolitan to her fingertips, and I'd back her to cope with awkward situations which you couldn't – "

He broke off to signal to his waiter, an Egyptian whose Western style tails and waiter's black tie were incongruous with his baggy trousers and scarlet tarboosh. He bowed low to Martha and was obsequious with Jude.

"*Effendi*, at your service," he said. "And the lady Troy – she is well, no?"

"Very well."

"But she is not with you tonight?"

"No." The curt tone of the monosyllable made an impertinence of the question, and the man murmured a perfunctory apology as he proffered the menu and summoned the wine waiter.

Jude chose European dishes – iced soup and steaks of white, firm-fleshed swordfish; a vol-au-vent, meltingly

97

rich, and the fresh fruit which was a luxury in Taroued, for dessert. He wasn't apologizing, he said, for dining no more imaginatively than they might have done in London or Paris or on the Riviera. In Taroued they were both at the mercy of tins and Arabian cooking, and he hoped Martha's palate would agree it could do with a change.

While they were drinking their coffee he asked the waiter what was the purpose of the outsize marquee which had been erected in the gardens, and was told that a troupe of travelling Bedouin dancers were performing there that night. "They should be worth seeing," he told Martha. "We'll go along, shall we?"

There was no charge for admission, nor much pretence of organized seating. Jude and Martha sat on one of the few cushioned benches at the side of the "stage", but for the most part the shifting audience chose to stand, moving diplomatically further afield when the collection tambourine went round, and drifting back again when it had passed.

The women dancers were unveiled and loaded with heavy amber and silver jewellery and, for all but the last dance of a long programme, wore their hair caught in filigree snoods. Every dance began on the same pattern – the men stamping and clapping on the outer circle, the women taking tiny backward steps on the inner. But always the interweaving of the circles which followed a change of tempo would be different, until all was a whirling kaleidoscope of colour and movement to the beat of a rhythm which had gathered speed to the point of frenzy.

During the interval while the collection was taken there was some clowning of sorts and a snake-charmer performed. Then the dancers reappeared, and the performance mounted to its climax of the traditional hair dance

of the women when, their heads flung back at an in-
credible angle, their knee-length black hair wove fantastic
circlings and figures-of-eight in the air.

Fascinated, Martha was sitting forward, watching this,
when a sixth sense told her Jude was not doing the same.

She glanced at him along the line of her shoulder. He
had shifted position on the bench so that he had her own
profile in full view and he was looking at her, not the
dancers, in a way which brought a tide of colour into
her cheeks.

"You're not watching!" she accused him.

"I've seen it all before." He glanced briefly at the
swaying figures of the women, their wreathing hair, then
looked back at her. "No, I was watching you instead.
In the face of novelty you're apt to go so wide-eyed with
wonder that it's good to entertain you, Martha – d'you
realize that?"

Embarrassed, she caught at a phrase. "Apt to . . . ?"
she quoted. "How do you know? This is the first time
we –"

"But not the first time I've been there to see when
you've marvelled at visions. For instance, Seiyid Alim's
reception – what about that?"

"Oh, there I admit I positively *goggled*!" she laughed.
"Who wouldn't have?"

"Not everybody. Of our own circle, Naomi, for one,
could never be so transparent, and Dorrit Randall is
at the age when it's 'square' to appear impressed. Whereas
you – well, when you glow unashamedly, you're well
worth watching, believe me." He glanced again at the
dancers, now drifting one by one from the stage. "This
will be the end," he said. "Shall we go?"

He held for her the sleeved stole she was carrying,
gesturing to her to put it on, and they walked back to his
car. "The night is still young. Would you care to go

somewhere and dance?" he suggested.

Martha shook her head. "Not unless you want to. After the dancing we've just seen, I should feel I'd got two left feet."

Jude nodded. "I know what you mean. Eastern limbs and bodies do so much more in the way of acrobatics and undulation that it's hard to credit they are articulated as ours are. All right, then, we'll go back to the harbour for another look at the sea."

He parked the car near where Martha had sat on the previous afternoon. The quays were quiet and deserted now, the sea a smooth black floor in which the riding-lights of the craft in the bay and the high stars found reflection. One of the dhows was dark and without sign of life aboard. The other, its sails hoisted and swelling, was lighted all along its length and echoing with activity, and as they watched it drew anchor and majestically put out to sea.

"What is the limit of its journey south?" Martha asked.

"Probably Mombasa or Zanzibar, and it will come back six months hence on the opposite monsoon. Anyway, how is your distance sight? Who is going to be able to spot it longest – no cheating, cross your heart?"

"Cross my heart – " For a long time she sat tense, straining her eyes, more than once ready to acknowledge defeat when the ship changed course and she lost its lights, and finally giving Jude best when she could see nothing and he could still describe what he saw.

"There . . . It's only a pinpoint, I admit. But – *there* . . . No? Then I win. Agreed?"

"You win." Her echo was faint, absent. As he had pointed out to sea his lifted hand had brushed her shoulder, and for the third time of being alone with him and knowing the same longing, she was fighting the prickle of nervous excitement, the quickened heartbeat, the caught breath that signalled the onset of a hunger she could not admit to him.

Greg would have understood it; their electric moments had rarely had need of words. At a touch even as casual or accidental as Jude's upon her arm, she could have turned to Greg and her lifted mouth could have said, "Kiss me – " as plainly as if she had spoken. And Greg, his desire sparking to meet hers, would have kissed her, seeking and sharing the sensation of oneness, of belonging, which from the very depth of her being she craved to know again. *But not* – the realization was as sharp as a knife-thrust under her heart – *not now at Greg Ryder's hands. At Jude's . . .*

Afterwards she wondered that she could have had the thought without making some movement, some betraying glance at him. But for all her ache to look at him, to see him in the new, blinding light of loving him for what he was and would be, even when he had gone on and away from her, her control held, and when, on a drawn-out "Well – " which she read as his full stop to their evening, he switched on and swung the car about, she was almost mistress of herself again.

But not quite. On the drive back she volunteered remarks, answered his. But only with an effort and in taut, few words, her mind not with her tongue; ranging instead over the mingled wonder and despair of loving again, yet of loving a man who would always put his work before marriage and who saw love itself as a trammelling curb, an intrusion he refused to tolerate.

Beneath the level of the cursory talk they exchanged she had time to marvel that she had taken so long to know that she had not been craving Greg's image in him, but him in himself; time to try to stifle the memory of Naomi's ugly inference – that he was content to substitute brief affairs without past or future for the kind of enduring love which should be enriched by both. Then – too soon or not soon enough? – they reached the hospital, and the evening was over.

They passed the night porter's booth and went through into the annexe where her ground-floor room was. Jude opened the door of the darkened corridor which led to it, and, feeling that it was someone else speaking with her voice, she turned to him to say goodnight.

"You've given me a lovely evening. I don't know how to thank you," she said.

He did not release the hand she had held out to him. "No?" he queried lightly. "But I've enjoyed it too, and isn't there supposed to be a time-honoured way for two people to thank each other on such occasions, without obligation on either side?"

She stared at him, her eyes dark. "A – ?" Her mouth went suddenly dry. She could not go on.

"Well, surely?" he said. "This – " But as his hands went to her shoulders, drawing her to him, and he bent to brush her cheek with his lips, suddenly the thing was out of hand for them both.

She was in his arms and they were clinging together in a kind of drowning urgency. He mutttered something thickly. It could have been "Martha – !" on a note of desperate appeal. Then his hands were rough about her hair, the line of her jaw, her throat, and again on her back, pressing the yielding curve of her body to the tautness of his own.

Unable to break out of the prison of his arms, she knew she did not want to, nor to question the torrent of passion which spoke in his searching lips and in the response of her own, answering kiss for kiss. While his need, however passing, however induced, matched her need of him, she could not count the cost of surrendering to it, of giving . . . and giving, with every fibre in her.

But that was only while she was allowing feeling to engulf her and sensation to do her thinking for her. Beyond and aloof, sanity waited to take over, and at last – after moments or an aeon? – it did.

She turned her head aside and thrust back hard against his arms in a silent protest she would have given worlds not to make. But he did not release her at once. Still holding her, he looked at her as if he needed to get her face in focus (*"as if I were a stranger!"*) and before he let her go he tilted her chin and kissed her again. But differently now – coolly, lightly, making the very deliberation of it a denial, an erasing of all that had gone before.

She stood apart from him, putting shaking hands to her hair. "That . . . that wasn't – " she began.

"Either fair or wise of me?" he prompted.

"Well, nothing had led up to it, had it?"

"Nothing," he agreed. "Simply a hunger that took us both by the throat at the same time, though for different reasons, and you don't have to justify yours – they're your affair. As for mine" – he paused – "let's face it, I'm a very ordinary man, Martha. Do I have to put it more plainly than that?"

"No." She shook her head, thinking that, short of outright crudity, he could hardly have chosen a more pointed way of telling her that an impulse of passion beyond his control would have flared as readily for any woman, ordinarily desirable and near, as for her.

"Then I'm forgiven?" he asked.

"Yes." On a spurt of pride she added, "That is, if I'm forgiven too?"

"For what?"

"For – " The offensive word stuck in her throat. "Co-operating with enthusiasm, without meaning anything by it."

Dark as it was, she saw his eyes glint, go hard. "Of course," he said. "I told you – your motives are your own." He moved a step closer, but did not touch her. "Now go to bed, Martha – you're in no more danger from me. It happened, but it's finished. Or if it will help you to forget it – it never even began in any way either of us need remember."

Then he left her and did not look back.

During the night which had seemed far too long for her wakefulness, she had dreaded coming face to face with him in the morning. But she was to be saved that ordeal alone. While she was breakfasting there was a message from him to say that, having arranged for his overnight patient to be discharged early, he hoped to be on the road by nine o'clock at the latest, and when she went out to the car, both men were already in their seats.

Jude drove fast. The conversation was general and spasmodic until the man at his side began to drowse. Then Jude signalled to Martha in dumb-show that they should let him sleep, and neither spoke for a long time.

They did not stop until they reached the guard house, and then only briefly, and they were on the outskirts of Taroued by early afternoon. Earlier Jude had said he proposed to call in at the hospital, before dropping the other two at their respective quarters, and on arrival there he suggested that they wait in the car while he went in to check with Ben.

But Ben was on his way across the forecourt as Jude braked and they met within a few feet of the car.

"And am I glad you're here!" was Ben's greeting to his chief. "What d'you know? – this morning we had an emergency drop in on us – drop in *literally* out of the blue. Chap in a light plane – one of the Desert Locust

Control jobs – tried to make the airstrip at Base, and crashed at the perimeter, completely writing off the aircraft, but somehow not killing himself. They got him out and called me. Bags of bruises, shock and a compound fracture of the right tibia. We brought him in; I reduced it, with Naomi acting as anaesthetist, and he came round a few minutes ago. He isn't in traction yet. Will you come and have a look at him?"

"Yes, of course. What went wrong? And where is his own base?" Jude asked.

"Well, D.L.C. Headquarters are at Basra. But he came out from a base near Aden. We've radioed them that he's safe, and it'll be his headache, explaining what happened to their aircraft. Our chaps diagnosed some instrument trouble – he was way off course when he bumped."

"English? Or what?"

Ben nodded. "Yes, English. Young chap – "

Both men turned together and moved out of earshot as Jude put another question to Ben. But at Ben's answer Martha, watching, saw Jude's lips frame an incredulous "*What* – ?" before he left Ben standing and strode back to the car.

"You heard most of that?" he asked her.

"Yes."

"Then you'd better be in on the rest of it. Because, if Ben has got his facts right, I think you know this man. His name is Ryder, Gregson Ryder, and whether or not you want to see him again, since he's here I'm afraid you're going to have no choice."

"*Greg?*" Martha's stab of shock was a physical pain beneath her breastbone. "Greg!" she repeated. "It can't be!"

Jude shrugged. "Seems it could. It's not a common

105

name, and didn't you tell me your ex-fiancé was in the flying business?"

"Yes, but not – !"

Jude's reply was to open the door of the car for her.

CHAPTER VII

They left her alone with Greg. Between the forecourt and the ward Jude had put Ben in the picture and she had met Ben's astounded concern with a bemused shake of her head. And now, beyond the screens which surrounded Greg's bed, she could hear Jude's and Ben's voices in murmured consultation about him.

Jude's – "It means immobilization for weeks. But I suppose you haven't told him that?"

And Ben's – "He was in no state to care. But that's why I didn't want to immobilize him until you showed up. You can't spare him a ward bed all that time, and I was going to suggest, if it's O.K. by you, that we move him over to the spare room at my place and put him in traction there."

Jude's again – "Or ship him down to Bab Magreb by air."

And Ben's, objecting, "There's no aircraft operational at the moment, and I doubt if we ought to keep him out of traction until there's air transport for him. Meanwhile, what a turn-up, eh, his lighting in here of all places, and Martha without a clue?"

They moved away, and then she was really alone with Greg; with the moment of reality she had imagined countless times, only, now that she was living it, to want it no longer. Jude had taken Greg's place in her heart and, except for the memories they shared, she knew she was finished with Greg. As he, almost certainly married by now, must be finished with her.

He was not fully round from the anaesthetic. When Jahra, who had been sitting with him, had slipped out between the screens and Martha had taken her place, he seemed to recognize her without surprise. But the effort of focusing his eyes on her was too much for him; his only response to her quiet, "Hello, Greg," was an incoherent mutter, and then he was drifting away again into his private mists.

She waited. When he came round again his need was to drink, and as she bent to hold the feeding-cup for him he stated rather than asked, "You're Martha – how come?" But though his diction was clearer and his eyes less vague, she saw he was still too bemused either to grasp the "how come" of her being there or to explain the turn of events which had brought him there himself.

She said as much to Ben when he came back a few minutes later to tell her that when Jude returned from taking his dental patient home, they proposed to move Greg to Ben's quarters at once.

Ben agreed, "I didn't think you'd achieve much give-and-take with him as yet. Jude thinks we may find he's concussed as well as shocked. But he is your chap all right, isn't he? That is – oh hell, Martha, you know what I mean. He *was*?"

Martha said, "Yes, he's Greg. But you don't have to spare my feelings, Ben. It was over, and he was engaged to someone else before I left England. And that's something I wanted to check with you – do you suppose his wife is out here with him? Or if not, will she have been told about his crash?"

Ben's answering stare was blank. "His wife? He isn't married!"

"*Not?*"

"According to my gen, no. You understand, when I

108

got to him he was unconscious and has stayed that way until now. But the chaps who hauled him out and looked at his papers said he was down there as single, and over the radio his base confirmed it."

"I see." Martha thought it out. "Then that makes his next of kin his parents, so that if his base informs them, they'll pass on the news to his fiancée, I dare say."

Ben said, "Why, surely. Anyway, it's not our pigeon and not as if, on his present showing, his condition were critical. Did you know this other girl, by the way?"

"I'd met her." As she had done for Jude, Martha outlined what she had known of Greg's plans for marriage and a career, but agreed with Ben that they didn't seem to tie in with his present connections.

"Seems to be a gap somewhere," puzzled Ben. "I mean, if he was marrying money and setting up in charter work with his in-laws, I wonder what he's about now, doing common-or-garden routine flights for D.L.C.?"

"That's what I'm wondering too," said Martha.

She was not to learn for several days – the period of heavy sedation ordered by Jude for Greg to ease his gradual recovery from shock. Jude, attending Greg, was strictly clinical; he showed none of Ben's interest in Greg's affairs, and though he left it to Martha to arrange his nursing care, he told her Greg was not to be questioned nor encouraged to talk until he, Jude, gave permission.

He gave it on the fifth morning – through Dorrit, who passed it on to Martha when she went in to relieve her of duty.

"When he woke this morning he had snapped out of it, just like that," Dorrit reported of Greg. "Quite himself, full of beans, hungry and wanting to know how, when, where, why – the *earth*. I played possum until Jude looked in on his way to the hospital. But when he did he said it looked like the All Clear and to tell you that you and Greg can go into a huddle now if you want to."

"Go into a huddle! Jude's phrase – or yours?" asked Martha dryly.

"Oh well," Dorrit dismissed the quibble, "what he actually said was that now you were free to get the record straight. And when I told him it was mutual, that Greg could hardly wait to hear the why and the wherefore of your being here, he – Jude, I mean – said he'd have thought it was a bit late in the day for Greg to care what had happened to you. Which, come to think of it," added Dorrit thoughtfully, "is about the most unprofessional thing I've ever heard Jude say."

Greg was smoking when Martha went into his room. But at sight of her he stubbed out his cigarette on his bed-table ashtray, then swore beneath his breath when his pinioned leg prevented him from drawing himself upward without help.

"Confound the thing!" He scowled at the framework and weights which held his leg immobile. "How long, for goodness' sake, have I got to stay trussed up like this?"

"Probably about three weeks more. After that we'll get you up and put you into walking plaster." Martha went to help him up and to plump his pillows. As she stood back – "Well, Greg?" she smiled at him.

He wrinkled his nose at her. "Well, Martha!" he mimicked. "Cue for 'This is so sudden', surely? So will you say it or shall I?"

"You can, if you like. I said it – or words to that effect – five days ago when you first dropped in, and since then I've got quite used to seeing you around. Sometimes taking an interest, sometimes not, but – around," she told him.

"Around? Doped to the eyebrows, flat on my back and with one leg in the air like a petrified ballet dancer? 'Around' is good, I will say!" Greg paused, then held out a hand to her. "But seriously, Martha, how come? You in this set-up, I mean? Tell All!"

She told him, answered the eager questions with which he broke into her story and then asked diffidently, "How is – Diana?"

Greg reached for a fresh cigarette and lit it. "Diana? She isn't," he said shortly.

"Isn't?"

"Oh, she's well enough, as far as I know." He studied the glow of the cigarette. "What I meant was that she doesn't signify any more where I'm concerned. She and I were all washed up, finished, over three months ago."

"Oh, Greg, I'm sorry!" (Strange, that she could say it and mean it in all sincerity now.) "But – three months? That must have been quite soon after – "

He nodded. "Exactly. About a couple of months after our break-up and your leaving Meerstead. Cause and effect with a vengeance."

"Cause and effect? What do you mean?"

"Just that. By some side wind it got around to old man Morse that my courting Diana was the reason for our affair ending. He had me on the carpet about it; told me I needn't bother to lie, and when I took him at his word and didn't, he wouldn't play."

"But Diana was of age, wasn't she? He couldn't forbid you to marry her."

"He admitted that, but said, in the new circumstances, he wasn't losing much sleep over it. Then he let me have it – the 'new circumstances' were that he had reconsidered staking me to a partnership in the charter-flight company, and if Diana still wanted to marry me, he'd see she understood the consequences."

"And Diana . . . didn't?"

"What do you think – that I gave her a chance?" Greg scoffed.

"You couldn't have helped yourself if you loved her. You mean – you didn't?"

"Not in any way that mattered. Oh, she was good company and a looker, and if she was the price of her old man's backing, that was all right by me. I liked her well enough, and we could have jogged along in marriage on money. But not without it. She was a snob of the first water, and once she found she was getting nowhere fast on what I could earn without capital behind me, we'd have been finished in a month. So I cut my losses and faded out. And as eighteen months' idling at home and two broken engagements hadn't exactly added to my popularity with my own old man, I took the first job that offered – which happened to be flying insecticide-spraying aircraft for Desert Locust Control."

"Is it a good job? Do you like it?" Martha asked.

Greg shrugged. "So-so. The pay is good – it'd better be, for all this 'he-man against Nature' stuff without any light relief. It was all right at the Basra H.Q. where I was while I got the hang of the spraying business. There were some girls around and more than a spot of night life to be had. But at my present base there's nothing but hangars, aircraft, one's own sex *ad nauseam* and a flying-rota system that might have been designed to keep a chain gang nose down. And by that token, believe it or not, I've only had one twenty-four hours' leave in Aden since I arrived. What's your own playground when you get a spell off duty here, by the way?"

"People go from here to Aden too, though more often

to Bab Magreb, which is nearer. But I haven't rated any leave yet, only hours and single days off duty, and the one time I have been down to Bab Magreb was to donate blood at the hospital," Martha told him.

"But you play here? Somewhere? With someone? You *must*! I mean, even if I was fool enough to jilt you and you got hurt, you can't have gone as dedicated as all that!" he protested.

She flushed. "Don't make a sneer of 'dedicated', please. It ought to be a lovely word. It *is*. And if I don't play much, as you call it, it's not because I've been eating out my heart for you, don't think it," she retorted.

Greg put a forefinger to his nose and made a scenting motion in the air. "Aha," he said, mock sagely, "do I sense a new romance – or do I? There's some lucky chap who's snaffled you on the rebound from me, and the next thing I'll know I'll be best man at your wedding?"

"No!"

"No?" At her sharp monosyllable his knowing smile faded. "Sorry, Martha dear. When you came back at me just now I thought you meant it and that you could take a joke about us. But that was just pride, was it, and you *were* hurt more than I knew?"

She looked at him, wondering that he could be obtuse enough to ask. "I shouldn't have wanted to marry you if I hadn't loved you. So naturally I was hurt. But if you didn't know how much, I'm glad. Because it hasn't lasted and I have got over it now," she told him, then smiled. "No pack drill, Greg! We've met again by the sheerest chance, but really we're only part of each other's past, aren't we?"

"But we needn't be any longer! I've admitted I was a fool to let you go, but we *have* met again and we're

113

both still free. And if this isn't the present, what is?"

Martha shook her head. "Not for us. We're finished – in that way."

"You mean – *you're* finished? You're through with me?"

"Yes, Greg."

"I don't believe it. As long as some other man hasn't swept you off your feet since, I can't mean *nothing* to you already. Why, five months ago you loved me enough to marry me – remember?"

"And five months ago you jilted me for Diana Morse," she reminded him.

She told herself she should have guessed his self-esteem would reject the logic of that. He said, "I've told you, I didn't love Diana. I – got embroiled, that was all. And if I did matter to you as much as you say, I could again. So what about giving me the chance to prove it to you, eh?"

"I'm afraid you couldn't now. I'm sorry, but it isn't there to prove any longer."

He grimaced. "You don't pull your punches, do you? And yet I wonder? For instance, if I kissed you now, shouldn't that tell us both how much there is left between us?"

Martha frowned. "Please don't, Greg. There'd be no point in it."

"All the same – " Suddenly, with an effort which she thought his position would prevent him making, his arm drew her down to him and he found her mouth in a kiss which the resistance of her lips kept as hard, brief and meaningless as a distant salute. After it, as if his male pride were piqued by her coldness, he continued to hold her stubbornly, then let her go.

He shook his head. "And how right you were, at

that! You *have* forgotten what kissing is for!" he accused her.

The gesture of her knuckles on her lips was one of wiping his kiss away. "Yes," she said. "And it was a mistake to try to make me remember."

"I don't know so much about that." He lay back and looked at her appraisingly from beneath his lashes. "I've always held that it's something you never really unlearn – like riding a bicycle. So don't worry. You used to know, and you will again. You're only out of practice – "

He broke off as, at the same instant as Martha did, he realized they were no longer alone. Jude was at the door, coming in.

He glanced from one to the other, then said to Martha,

"I've brought Dorrit back to stand by here. I want you for another job." Then to Greg, "I've got someone along to see you – your chief from your Aden base. He contacted me first to check on how you were and whether you could be seen, and if you're equal to it, he'd like a talk with you."

Greg hesitated. "You mean I'm supposed to see him now?"

Before he replied Jude went to take his pulse. When he had done so he said, "Well, there's no reason there why you shouldn't. And though it's for you to say, if you refuse he'll have made the flight for nothing and will want to come again, I daresay."

Greg said distastefully, "*Questions – !*" And then, "Oh, all right, wheel him in." He offered cigarettes to Jude, who refused, then looked at Martha above the flame of his lighter. "See you again soon, honey chile? I mean, we've still got quite a bit of leeway to make up, haven't we?"

Martha froze at his implication that there remained hours' worth of eager exchange for them to share. Hating also the thought that, unless Jude gave a hint that he had witnessed Greg's kiss, she could hardly buttonhole him to explain how reluctant had been her part in it, she answered Greg with an unnecessary stiff promise that she would look in on him later and ignored his murmured gibe of "Can you beat that? Just how professional can we get at the drop of a hat?" as she went ahead of Jude out of the room.

Jude went back to show in the D.L.C. man, then rejoined her to tell her that Will Shorthouse, the Company's second air pilot, had reported sick with a recurrence of an earlier thrombosis condition of the leg. Jude was warding him in his quarters for a few days' observation before sending him down to Bab Magreb, and Martha's assignment was to see him into bed and comfortable when Ben, who had seen Will at Base, brought him over from there.

Jude had Will's key from Will's housemate, and when they reached the bungalow, he went in with Martha, saying he would wait as well to see Will settled. Meanwhile – after a glance at the cluttered room both men shared – could Martha give it something more of the quality of a sickroom, did she suppose?

Martha agreed that she could, and did, tidying away clothes, sports gear, paperbacks, dusting and making up both beds with fresh linen. Finishing while there was still no sign of her patient's arrival, she gave the kitchen some badly needed attention and then went to join Jude in the living room.

"All set?" He looked at his watch. "Ben must have been delayed." He motioned Martha to the window seat and stood beside her with a knee on the low sill, watching the road.

She asked him to brief her more fully on Will's case and he did so. Then he said casually, "Well, do I take it you've been able to fill in some of the gaps in Ryder's recent history which were puzzling you?"

Half relieved, half sorry that the question gave no clue as to whether or not he had eavesdropped on her last minute or two alone with Greg, Martha said, "Yes. It makes sense now. He tells me that soon after I left England his plans for joining the charter company I told you about came to nothing, and so he took this job with Desert Locust Control instead."

"Which wipes out, of course, the apparent coincidence of his arrival here. Yes, well, I've been put in so much of the picture too – by Captain Lessop, his chief, who is with him now. But didn't you tell me originally that Ryder was, so to speak, marrying into the charter flight business?" asked Jude.

Martha said again, "Yes. But he isn't married; he isn't going to be. He tells me his engagement fell through too."

Jude lifted a brow. "He ought to watch it. Breaking engagements could grow on him. Or wasn't he the guilty party in the collapse of this one?"

"I don't know," she lied, out of an old loyalty to Greg which had always been ready in his defence against implied criticism. "I suppose, if they both realized in time that they had made a mistake, there needn't have been any question of blame. But after that, for Greg to go into partnership with Diana Morse's brother would have put him in an impossible position. One can see that."

"One can indeed," Jude agreed smoothly. "And naturally it would be slanderous to wonder aloud which may have folded first, the lucrative job or the engagement – " He broke off and nodded through the window. "Here are Ben and our patient at last. I'd like you to get Will to bed straight away; then stay with him, will you, until his housemate gets back?"

Jude kept her mainly on observation of Will Short-house until he was flown to Bab Magreb for further treat-ment. In consequence she saw Greg only briefly, and it was not until some days later that she heard from him the outcome of his chief's visit.

When she went into his room he was frowning over a letter which he at once flicked across to her with an exclamation of disgust.

"Read that!" he raged. "And they say honesty pays! I came clean with Lessop, and what do I get for my pains? The push! All I can say is, it's lucky for them I don't want their wretched job. Because if I did, they'd find themselves being sued for breach of contract just as soon as I could beat it to a lawyer's office!"

Martha read. The letter was a formal dispensing with his further services and an offer of three months' salary in lieu of notice, to date from the ending of his convales-cence. Handing it back to him, Martha said, "That's tough, Greg. *Had* you a contract with D.L.C. that they're breaking by writing this?"

"Not really. There was just this agreement of three months' notice on either side," he admitted.

"Then they're within their rights, aren't they? But why are they dismissing you? You were on a routine flight for them when you crashed, weren't you?"

"Of course not. Spray aircraft don't operate singly. The muster is usually half a dozen at least, strung out more or less wing to wing, like a lot of game beaters. No, I'd got fed up and had sloped off on a bit of a joy-ride. But I didn't make any secret of it to Lessop. Other chaps were doing it all the time on the station, and how was I to know I'd picked a crate that was due in dock with instrument trouble? I didn't try to crash the thing; it ditched me. And if I'd had the ordinary luck to take it back whole, Lessop need never have been the wiser that I'd had it out."

"Oh, Greg!" Realizing she had always least liked him when he resorted to bluster or injured innocence to his own defence, Martha added sharply, "Well, clean breast to Captain Lessop or no, you did crash their plane on a truant flight, and you could hardly expect them not to fire you, if only to make an example of you. But it's a pity. I'm sorry. And I suppose you can hardly ask them for a reference now?"

Greg scoffed, "Ask them? Can you see me? Anyway, my best reference is built-in – I happen to be a damn good pilot for anyone's money, and a lot can happen in three months plus, before I'm on the dole." He crumpled the letter, took accurate aim for the wastepaper basket, then indicated his suspended leg. "D'you know Tarleton says I've still done only about half my time in this contraption?"

Martha nodded. "Yes. But once you're in plaster you'll be able to get about, and by Christmas I daresay you can be off as soon as you please."

"Always supposing I want to be off the minute I'm mobile. From all I hear – I've seen nothing for myself – this isn't much of a dump, but it could have been worse, and I'm not grumbling. Besides – Christmas? What are you laying on for it, do you know?"

"Nothing much, I expect, as it doesn't mean to the Bedouins all that it does to us Europeans. There's to be Morning Service at Base, I think, and I suppose we may foregather in someone's quarters in the evening."

"To carouse and wassail on claret cup in paper hats? I can hardly wait. That is, I couldn't if I hadn't had a lot better idea. For instance, that you and I leave the rest of them to it and hop down to Aden or Bab Magreb on our own. What do you say?"

"No!" Martha covered her recoil from the bittersweet of her memories of Bab Magreb by adding quickly, "That is, I imagine the routine here will be much as usual, and the oilmen are bound to be given priority on any plane going down to the coast. Besides, you may not be here yourself. After all, Ben and Dorrit Randall only put you up because there was no way of moving you to hospital quickly enough on the day you crashed, and you can hardly expect them to keep you as a guest once you're convalescent."

"Then if I'm not to outstay my welcome I'd better malinger a while, hadn't I? Avoid appearing too convalescent too soon?" suggested Greg.

"You could always try malingering with Jude Tarleton and see where it would get you," Martha told him dryly.

He nodded. "Yes, I see your point. Not strong on the sympathetic bedside manner, your worthy Chief. Or is it, I wonder, that for some reason I'm not his favourite boy? However, even he can hardly throw me out at Christmastime, with a gammy leg and no job to go to this side of Suez. So don't be in too much of a hurry to kiss me goodbye, Martha dear, because, to quote you, I could be around for quite some time yet!"

As Martha had forecast, there was something of a mass exodus from the base camp over Christmas, leaving only a handful of European personnel behind after every motorized vehicle had been pressed into service and David Sellers had flown shuttle, day after day, carrying parties of men down to Bab Magreb and to Aden.

She had been equally right that it was business as

usual – or more so – in the clinic and the hospital. For Christmas week brought the sudden onset of the desert's bitter winter; short, but savage while it lasted, and already demanding its cruel toll of the undernourished by way of the bronchitis and influenza which at that season took over from cholera and heatstroke and malaria as killers.

The wards filled up again; outside visits to patients had to brave the twin hazards of icy winds and dust-storms, and in a scene which might have been set for the Nativity itself, Christmas dawned as unheralded as any other working day.

For Martha it passed without personal incident. Jude gave her time off for the Christmas morning service and there she briefly felt something of its spirit. But she went straight back to duty, and the evening party of sorts proved only an affair of relays – Jude dropping in on it while Ben stood in for him; the girls doing the same for each other, and the whole thing breaking up before mid-night for want of festive feeling enough to keep it going under such handicaps.

Meanwhile Martha's fears of Greg's straining Tar-oued's hospitality seemed unfounded.

He and Ben struck a casual friendship, and he teased Dorrit boyishly on the teenage level she understood best. He flirted and sparred with Naomi on equal terms, and only he and Judy kept the distance of men who recognized they had so little in common that they would still remain acquaintances after ten years together on a desert island. As soon as he began to get about he spent most of his time at the base camp and sometimes flew with David Sellars. He appeared to have no present plans for moving on and Martha believed herself the only person in their set who would be relieved to see him go.

Detachedly she watched him radiating the easy,

spurious charm which until now had always disarmed her judgement of him. She suspected Ben, Dorrit, Naomi, everyone, had heard only a carefully edited version of his ill-luck in both his career and his love affairs, and she knew, none better, how convincingly he could paint himself as the innocent victim of an unkind fate.

She sometimes thought how the current word "phony" matched him. But she was reluctant to label him aloud with it. She must allow him the right to make his own impression, she told herself, and when he did go, as before long he must, she supposed the small world of Taroued would forget him as quickly and finally as she now could herself.

But in counting the days to his departure she was to find she had reckoned without the resource and powers of self-salesmanship of which he had boasted to her.

Early in January, at Jude's cool hint that Ben and Dorrit now had enough to do without continuing to play host to him, he had sought and gained the permission of the camp manager to move into Will Shorthouse's empty quarters. And a fortnight later, to Martha's rank dismay, he was offered Will's job as second pilot to David Sellars; her first news of this coming to her from Jude as he was driving her to visit a case on the outskirts of the town.

Of the camp manager's intention to offer Greg the vacancy Jude told her, "In fact, Dumont was going to sound Ryder today. But he'll wait now until I give him the word to go ahead. And whether I do or not," not looking at her, he paused, "depends on you."

"On *me*?"

"On *you*," he confirmed. "Dumont doesn't and needn't know why I asked him to stall, but it seemed to me we ought to get your reactions first."

"To a Company appointment I couldn't possibly influence? Or which surely you can't either?" Martha queried.

"Officially, no. Nor, if it were a question of a full contract, would the decision rest with Dumont. But in an emergency or for taking on a man for a trial term, he has *carte blanche*, and if I weigh in for or against Ryder, he'll listen to me."

Martha drew a long breath. "May I get this clear? You're suggesting that if I tell you I'd rather Greg didn't get the offer of Will Shorthouse's job, you can see that he won't get it? Or, vice versa, that he will?"

"That's about the shape of it, yes. The choice is yours; you can leave the rest of me. That is, if you decide against, I can offer Dumont quite valid medical arguments as to his unreadiness for the job. On the other hand, if you decide for, and he stays, among other things he'll be signing-on on the same terms as the rest of the Company's men with regard to the 'No wives, No fiancées along' clause in his contract, and I dare say you understand the implication of that?"

Stung by a hint of warning which she resented, Martha said, "As long as Greg understands it, that's all that matters, isn't it? Why make a point of it to me?"

She felt Jude's glance on her, but would not meet it. "I've an idea you must know," he said. "I was reminding you that you have much the same agreement with me. In your case, an unwritten one, but equally binding while you are here."

"Meaning that, now Greg is free, you think I'm in danger of getting involved with him again?"

Jude shook his head. "Voicing no opinion on the matter; merely pointing out obligations which you undertook and expecting you to honour them, that's all."

"You needn't worry. They'll be honoured," Martha

123

promised. "After all, I can't claim I haven't had fair notice of your attitude to emotional complications. Except, it seems," she added recklessly, "to certain kinds which don't happen to amuse me – "

"Just a moment. You suggest I turn a blind eye to – which kind?" he cut in.

"I'd say – to one-evening affairs which don't mean a thing to either side; to the bees-round-a-honeypot kind which Naomi thrives on and which you allow her all the time. Meanwhile, about Greg – we haven't any present intention of patching things up, but if we ever decided to, well, Monsieur Dumont would have his remedy and you would have yours, wouldn't you?"

She felt she had been driven to the insolence of that, but if she expected a violent reaction from Jude she got none. He agreed, "Exactly. I couldn't have put it better myself. And now, do I advise Dumont that our friend stays or goes?"

"Neither – on my say-so, please. You've no right to put such a decision on to me," she protested.

He shrugged. "I'm sorry. I thought you might see it as a kindness. But forget it. Dumont needs him, so I daresay you may conclude he'll be staying."

"May I? But how do you know Greg himself will agree to?" she flashed perversely.

Jude said, "I don't. But won't he?" It was not a question. It was an end to the conversation.

CHAPTER VIII

With a word she could have been rid of Greg. And yet she had not uttered it. Why? Martha wondered later.

Because, she argued, to have been given the choice of whether he went or stayed had outraged her sense of justice. She had no right, she told herself, as she had told Jude, to order Greg's immediate future in such a way. But she knew that her resentment had also sparked to Jude's assumption that both Greg and she must be warned against taking up the threads of their intimacy while Greg was in the employ of the Company.

If only Jude knew how little she needed warning! And if only her defences against his indifference hadn't been hammered so hard and high that she could have said something like, "Greg means nothing to me now. I'd rather he went away, but I'm not afraid of his staying," and let him read what he would into that!

But pride had made her say just the opposite. Pride – and perhaps a queer, warped notion that she could best live down her love for Jude by keeping her distance from him; yielding no personal inch to him and hiding her secret beneath an outward composure which matched his own.

It was not easy. In the same room she could not keep her eyes from straying to him, watching him; his name, spoken aloud, had the power to send her heart plunging, and at the sight of his hands at work, cool, capable, deft, she ached to surrender again to a strength and urgency which she knew they had, if only in an impulse of passion which had been for him a thing of a moment – no more.

Meanwhile she had had to pretend unconcern at Greg's acceptance of Will Shorthouse's job. In announcing it to her his own attitude had been summed up in his cavalier, "Easy. The job was going; I was free and, Dumont admitted that he would be a fool to let me slip through his fingers." Whereupon she left him to think it had been as "easy" as all that, bit back the impulse to remind him that, lacking references after his record with D.L.C., he was lucky to be given the offer, and silently vowed to force Jude to witness how little Greg meant to her now, how little she meant to him.

It was Greg who did not make the latter easy. Whenever there were other men present, he hinted at his claim on her. "Martha and I . . ." "Ah, I know Martha too well . . ." "D'you remember, Martha, that night when we . . . ?" By such phrases, by a hand tucked beneath her arm or flung companionably across her reluctant shoulders, he tried to state his possession of her, driving her to every kind of subtle tactic to avoid him. Fortunately his working hours kept him at the base camp or flying, and in the evenings when he was free, she frequently returned to the hospital for duty.

So the January and February days climbed towards a spring which came suddenly with a dropping of the wind, a new warmth to the sun and a brief flowering of wild iris, short-stemmed hyacinth and a few hardy grasses sprouting between the rocks alongside the desert tracks.

It came to the base camp with the renewal of the seismic soundings which had been held up by the winter. It came to the market-place with the day-long sunning and gossiping of the old men. It came with lambs in the sheepfolds, young to the camels and the few lean mares, and in the way it has the world over, it set love defying locksmiths in the hospital itself. Ahmadi, doing dressings and doling out pills, was looking at Mina and finding her pleasing, and Mina, making beds and serving diets, was looking in her turn – though pretending that she wasn't.

Martha and Dorrit watched the progress of the romance with all their feminine interest. Ahmadi, hovering about the clinic, making unnecessary jobs for himself, meant that he hoped to be sent on an errand to the wards. Mina, blandly urging Jahra or Nura to go ahead of her off duty, meant that she intended to grant Ahmadi a brief rendezvous in the sunshine of the forecourt. There were also days when her caprice of the moment kept the two younger girls clamped as closely to her side as if the three of them were handcuffed together. Thus bodyguarded, she looked through Ahmadi as if he did not exist, and then Ahmadi's work suffered until her mood passed and her dark eyes saw him again.

He never tried similar strategies with her. His devotion was continuous and absolute, and gradually Mina melted to it. But at the point where Dorrit was ready to prophesy that he and Mina would be "going steady" from then on, one day Martha came upon Mina in the cloakroom, weeping as she changed into her duty overall and refusing at first to tell Martha why.

During the few minutes of her sympathetic questions which went unanswered, Martha wondered whether it was possible that Jude had brought his iron veto to bear on the warm little romance. He knew of it, of course, it had escaped no one in or around the hospital. But surely, *surely* – ! Martha was near to praying when suddenly Mina raised tear-suffused eyes to hers, said obscurely, "I am no one," before she dissolved again.

Martha said gently, "How do you mean, you are no one? You are Mina bint Kahder – Mina, the daughter of Kahder. Doesn't bearing your father's name make you someone, even though he and your mother are dead?"

But Mina would not have that. She was no one because she had no one of her own, she insisted. Nobody to whom Ahmadi's parents could broach the question of his betrothal to her; nobody whose place and right it was to conduct the shrewd barter for her without which Ahmadi could not marry her, even if she had anything to bring him as her dowry, which she had not.

"But if Ahmadi loves you and will take you without a dowry, is that not enough?" asked Martha in the precise English which Mina understood.

Seemingly it was not enough. Even though Ahmadi might choose his own bride, his father would expect to go through the ritual of asking her hand of someone who sponsored her and who could promise that silver or its equivalent value in sheep or grain would go with her.

Martha thought. "Your landlady, Kalifa Fatma – she would speak for you?" she suggested.

"She is a woman and a widow. She may not speak for a girl."

"Her brother, then? He is a good man with daughters of his own. Would he not speak for you to Ahmadi's father?"

Doubtfully Mina admitted that he might, and that if he would the proprieties could be taken as observed. But for Kalifa Fatma's nieces there would be dowry. Whereas for her –

"Leave that to me. It may be arranged," Martha promised with more confidence than she felt. The only person she knew who might smooth matters for Ahmadi and Mina was Jude, and she had no wish to ask favours of him just now. But she had no choice. She had promised Mina. So when she knew him to be alone in his office she knocked at the door and went in.

"If you can spare me some time, I wanted to speak to you about Ahmadi and Mina," she began.

He stood, turning a chair towards her. "Yes?" he invited. And then, dryly, "Quite a problem they've set us, haven't they? Perhaps we'd better pool our ideas, eh?"

She looked at him in surprise. "Oh, you know about it, then?"

"Ahmadi unburdened his soul to me yesterday. To you too?"

"No. I came on Mina having a quiet weep and got the story from her. What does Ahmadi propose to do, do you know?"

"There's not much he can do while his father has his heels well dug in against Ahmadi's proposing marriage to an orphan with no one in her background to conduct the appropriate business for her."

"Yes, well, I did have an idea about that," put in Martha.

"You did? What is it?"

She told him, watched him consider it in silence, then added, "And I had some vague notion that we could have a whip-round amongst ourselves and the oilmen for a dowry for Mina. I don't know how much she would need."

"Less than you would expect by our standards. But it's not as good a plan as your idea for a sponsor for her. These are proud folk, and they mustn't smell a hint of charity. It would be better if I approached the Company for a gratuity for her. Then, if the Superintendent of the Bab Magreb school would play, he might put it over that he had been holding money in trust for her against her marriage. How would that do?"

"Splendidly, I'd say." Martha paused, then raised candid eyes to his. "You know, when I came to see you, I hardly expected to find you so helpful about all this," she said.

"Why not? Ahmadi's romance has to be resolved one way or another if he's to keep his mind on his job; this last week or two it's been a dead loss. But I suppose, in view of our last brush on the subject of – what was it? – 'emotional complications', you were prepared for obstructions from me?"

"I – hoped not."

"But you expected otherwise. My dear girl," Jude moved a hand impatiently, "do appreciate, will you, how little comparison there is? Ahmadi is a desert-born Arab who needs to state his very manhood by the number of sons he has, and Mina, who is already nearly seventeen, could have been betrothed at twelve and married a year or two later. A Bedouin girl's one destiny is marriage, and I remember telling you I was prepared for a fairly swift turnover in nursing aides when I took these three on."

Martha said, meaning it, "I'm sorry. I admit I was afraid you might stand in her way. See it as your duty, I mean."

"You could, of course," he returned dryly, "give me credit for being a realist, rather than a monster of unreason. We needn't lose Ahmadi, and though, after her marriage, Mina will melt into her background of domesticity and in-laws, she will take with her the leaven of all she has learned here about child-care and hygiene, just as Jahra and Nura will too, when their turn comes. Meanwhile, I hope I've persuaded you of the world of difference between them and you and Naomi, both of you free agents with careers at your fingertips if you shouldn't marry, which of course you will. *And* between

Ahmadi and the men of the Company, signing on as bachelors and grass widowers for the time they are out here on soundings?"

"Yes," Martha allowed. "But would it be such a bad thing to permit them their wives here, do you think? After all, Ben's marriage works, and if his does, why shouldn't the others'?"

"It works now, thanks largely to you. But it hung for a lot too long on the thread of Dorrit's discontent, and multiply that by a hundred or so women hankering for hair appointments and the sales and TV, and you have your answer as to the Company's wisdom in banning wives," he countered.

"That's rather sweeping, isn't it? If they have to, the majority of women can take primitive conditions just as well as men!"

"Maybe. But they shouldn't be asked to, unless their work is contributing to the community, and that not indefinitely. For instance Naomi's contract with us expires next month, and unless she elects to renew it, she'll be free to move on. You too, when you've put in your year for which I engaged you."

"That will be in July. But supposing I wanted to, could I stay on too?" Martha asked.

"If we're likely to go on being operational and you're prepared to accept much the same terms of contract as now, certainly. But a lot can happen between now and July, and I think we'd better postpone talking about it until then."

On that, adding his promise that he would look into the matter of Mina's dowry, he went to open the door for her in dismissal.

The possibility of Naomi's departure had been complete news to Martha. But as they rarely discussed any but their daily plans she did not mention it until Naomi did so herself. Then she told her she had heard of it earlier from Jude, adding, "I hadn't realized until then that there was a limit to your time here. But are you really thinking of going?"

"Probably." Naomi lit a cigarette and inhaled lazily. "What is there to stay for? If they don't strike oil, and if Seiyid Alim refuses to play, the whole thing collapses. And don't quote rats leaving the sinking ship, because in these circumstances any wise rat would."

"And if you do leave, where will you go?"

"Somewhere. Anywhere. I've got some feelers out and here and there I've made contact. Beirut. Cairo. Or further afield – America, North or South."

"You sound very footloose," Martha commented. "But haven't you found your work here satisfying enough? For instance, in your place I doubt if I *could* leave without knowing the result of all the research that Ben is still working on."

Naomi said, "I can bear the thought, and I daresay Ben will find someone else to pass him test-tubes and the litmus paper when he wants them."

"You know you do much more than that in the lab and for the whole set-up," Martha protested.

"Perhaps. But I don't claim to make work my be-all and my end-all, even to please Jude. Anyway, I've found other ways of doing that."

"Have you?" Martha's tone was dry, non-committal.

Naomi regarded her through half-closed lids. "Well, I know you favour the 'life is real, life is earnest' approach yourself. But though you might suppose his veins ran distilled water in working hours, I assure you Jude is only human like the rest of us, and he has his moments, believe me."

"Speaking from experience of having 'got' him, as you

once boasted to Dorrit you could?"

"But naturally! Easy. Give him the choice of time, place and condition, and he really goes to town. But only if you accept his moments *as* moments, of course. Because Jude was the original model for that gag about love being for a man a thing apart, and any girl who hopes otherwise on a few passionate kisses from him is going to be disappointed – very."

"But do you," asked Martha carefully, "know of any girl around her besides yourself whom Jude has chosen to kiss in one of his 'moments' and who might need the warning?"

Naomi rose, stretched and sauntered towards her room. "Not on eye-witness evidence, no," she drawled. "Do *you*?"

Martha let her go, despising herself for inviting the retort by her own ill-judged question and resolving to be drawn into no more such verbal sparring while Naomi remained in Taroued.

Later the little community was to remember Mina's wedding day for more than it signified to the girl herself and to Ahmadi. But it dawned as just another golden spring day, with the difference that, for the first time in his service, Ahmadi was not on duty in the clinic and Mina was already installed in his father's house where, by Bedouin custom, the ceremony and the marriage feast would take place.

A week had sufficed for the delicate give-and-take between her sponsor and her future father-in-law, and, once both sides were satisfied, the day was fixed for a fortnight later, though with no formal bidding of guests. Ahmadi and Mina were married on the previous evening in the privacy of the family circle, and were already husband and wife when the dawn-to-dark ritual of feasting and dancing to the music of tambourines and drums began.

The family ate separately and more richly than the guests, who streamed in as by right to help themselves to the spread of rice and hard-boiled eggs and date pastries before giving place to the eager press of people behind them, crowding then into other rooms of the house, overflowing finally into a cramped courtyard, and so on their way.

Jude, who had promised Ahmadi he would be there, was not able to go. Two days earlier he had received a "command" summons to Aden from Sheikh Seiyid Alim; he had left the following day and was still there. Naomi excused herself on the score of being occupied with preparations for her leaving, but Ben, Dorrit and Martha went along together, joining the queue at noon and achieving the hospitality of the house quite a long time later.

Ahmadi, a little sheepish in his wedding garments of an indigo blue robe caught up at the waist above narrow embroidered trousers, was there with the men of his family. But Mina was not with him. In the interests of the fiction that bride and groom had not met until the ceremony and must not enjoy each other's company until after the twenty-four hours' celebrations, she was with the women in a room on the second floor, and Ben had to stay below when Martha and Dorrit went to pay their respects to her and her new in-laws.

Like Ahmadi, she was completely transformed from the Mina they knew.

She too wore blue over an underskirt of striped silk; her wedding headdress was a circlet of silver; her black hair was in innumerable tight plaits and she wore a gauze face-veil for the first time. Seated on a floor cushion surrounded by the older women, she looked happy and excited, but pathetically young and remote. When

Ahmadi's honeymoon was over, he would return to the Western world of his work at the hospital, but the East had already reclaimed Mina. She would keep Ahmadi's house and she would bear Ahmadi's children. But she would not again run free with Jahra and Nura, and Martha, congratulating her on her new dignity, could not but feel a pang of regret that it had to be so.

The girls stayed for a while to accept sweetmeats and to drink the ceremonial cup of tea which was offered. Then they rejoined Ben below, and after watching the dancing and drinking more tea, the three of them left to return to the hospital.

There, Jude's car was in the forecourt, and Jude himself was in the clinic. He was alone, and unlike him, was doing nothing. Hands in the pockets of his shorts, he stood beside his desk, looking down at it but not seeing it, Martha realized. And when, at Ben's careless, "So you're back, Chief? How was Aden and what did his Sheikhship want?" he glanced up and focused on Ben, she feared she could guess at the news which he had to tell.

She was right. Squaring his shoulders, he moved round the desk to sit at it. He spoke to Ben but his glance swept the three of them as he said stonily, "He wanted to tell me that, failing a 'strike', he doesn't intend to renew the Company's concession and, if and when it folds, he can't see his way to backing a medical service for Taroued thereafter."

"He won't? The old – !" Ben's epithet was unprintable, and Dorrit's, though milder in quality, was no less emphatic. Martha, aware of a curious shame at being forced to witness the haggard, stripped look on Jude's face, dragged her eyes away and said nothing.

Perhaps Ben felt the same. He moved to the open door and stood, speaking back over his shoulder. "You were banking a good deal on his Yes, Chief?"

"A good deal." Jude's tone made it the understatement it was.

"Does Murray know?"

"I haven't seen him since I got back, but he does now, through Seiyid Alim's official notice to the Company. Dumont too. It was by way of special courtesy that I was summoned to Aden to be told in person."

"I hope," said Ben, "you thanked the gentleman for nothing. What's the difficulty? Lack of cash?"

"More the *Inshallah* – 'Allah Wills It' philosophy, I gather. He acknowledged we had accomplished a lot and no doubt could do more, given the freedom of continued backing and time to do it in. But money-wise, if there's no oil find, he wants the Company out and somebody else in, at a higher price for the concession. Meanwhile we stay with his blessing, as long as we do so by any agency other than his. If we have to go – too bad. But if we do, there will still remain for his people the Providence which has cared for them for centuries – *Inshallah*."

"Locusts. Drought. Trachoma. Avoidable septicaemia. I'd hate to be the Providence answerable for that lot unaided," Ben murmured. "What did you say to all that?"

Jude shrugged. "Does it matter? You don't argue with the East and you don't wilfully make it the enemy of anything that's important to you. Besides, I'd already said it all – said it and lived it and shown it – or so I'd hoped."

"But had you, do you think – well enough?" It was Martha's voice, only half bidden by her will, which intervened.

Jude turned a cold glance on her. "Had I what – well enough?"

"I just wondered," she faltered, "whether the hospital did as much to impress the Sheikh as you hoped it might. If you remember, Dorrit and I weren't even in evidence on duty that day – "

"Forget it," he cut in. "It mattered at the time, but the issue doesn't, and never did, hang on a triviality like that. I've told you – Seiyid Alim admits everything we've achieved, denies nothing. The only thing he won't do is to lift a finger to help. Except in so far as he is prepared, he says, to make *you* the offer of a permanent job if and when the rest of us leave."

"*Me!* A job? In heaven's name, what as?" Martha exclaimed.

"As resident nurse to his younger children and to the four houses his religion allows him. I told him I doubted if you would be interested, but I promised to pass on the message all the same."

"But he never even saw me at work – just at his reception, that was all!"

"Apparently he was impressed by your fluency in Arabic, and still more by your life-saving effort that evening," Jude said.

"*You* made more of that to him than there really was to it," she told him as Ben returned from the doorway to tease her.

"Well, there you are, Martha – a chance to make your mark as another 'Anna and the King of Siam', while the rest of us go on the dole! Think of all the lovely lolly you'll get when you write your memoirs and begin to rake in the film rights – oh, my!"

She smiled at him, grateful to him for lessening the tension with the joke. "Sorry, Ben," she said. "No 'Secrets of the Harem' from me, I'm afraid. When I have to leave here, I shall be going back to England as I always planned I should."

"Which is where we're all likely to fetch up, come summer – eh, Chief?" Ben turned to address Jude.

Jude did not answer at once. Then, "*No!*" he said. And again, explosively, "No. Sheikh or no, Company or no, the hospital is here and here it's staying while there's one patient for a bed in it or one germ we haven't tracked to its source – " Standing, he strode round the desk to face Ben. "Well?" he challenged, as if daring Ben to demur at his peril.

Martha held her breath, knowing – as Jude surely must – that, short of a miracle, he hadn't a hope of implementing the threat, but loving him the more for the burning faith in his work which had driven him to the reckless, rearguard courage of it.

With every nerve she willed that Ben shouldn't quench the flame too soon. But Ben was married, he had Dorrit to think of, and he said, "All very well, Chief. But how long could you keep going with nothing coming in? We run on a shoestring as it is."

"I could do it on less if I had to."

"On less, but not on nothing."

"Who mentioned nothing? There are funds to be had somewhere. From U.N.O., the Red Cross, people of heart in England. We haven't had to beg anyone's charity yet, but I'm damned if I won't if all else fails – " Jude broke off as the young English-speaking Bedouin who manned the radio came in. "Yes, Abdel Tazar, what is it?" He took the paper which the boy proffered, read its message, then passed it to Ben.

"From Murray. So much for premature heroics, eh? Read it," he said.

Ben read and so did both girls, craning over his shoulder to do so. Jude watched them in silence, the corner of his mouth lifting in a quiet, withdrawn smile. The radioed message said,

Exploratories Numbers Three and Seventeen, thirty miles apart, both report extensive anticlines and strongest yet response to soundings. In other words – two strings to our bow. Drilling begun at each site. Not home and dry by long chalk yet, so keep all fingers crossed and don't start counting chickens.

Dorrit read aloud, making a marvel of every word; Martha, hardly trusting the news they had awaited so long; Ben re-read, then handed the paper back to Jude and grinned, "Trust a ca'canny like Murray senior to spring something like this and then to soft-pedal on it like crazy! But fighting through his bag of mixed metaphors, wouldn't you say he knows very well that this is it and that they're bound to find on one or both these sites?"

Jude nodded. "He knows, I think."

Ben agreed. "My guess too that he's as cocksure as any good Scot allows himself to get. So – where can we hope to go from here?"

"Nowhere spectacular at once. Just into a future we didn't know we'd got five minutes ago," said Jude.

The base camp's immediate and logical reaction to its break-through was to throw a celebration party. It was planned for the night of the day on which the first drilling rig struck certain oil, which happened at Number Three Camp a fortnight later.

That was a day or two after Naomi was due to leave. But though Dorrit prophesied sourly that she would cash in on the new situation and decide to stay on after all, she merely postponed her departure in order to take in the party, before flying down to Aden the next day.

On the evening of the party Jude and Ben were to divide duty, Jude going over to the camp for the first hour or two and returning later to take over from Ben at the hospital. Martha and Dorrit were free to go together, but Martha was to leave with Jude in order to sleep "on call" for the rest of the night.

Dorrit was still dressing when Martha went to call for her, and as she sat with her while she did so, Martha was struck by how Dorrit had changed over the months of their friendship.

She had lost most of her puppy fat and, with it, a lot of her gaucherie. She cared now how she dressed and was even willing to sew for herself with Martha's help. She took trouble with the little make-up she used and, at Martha's suggestion, had abandoned her tortured pony-tail for a softer, layered cut which framed her face.

Tonight especially there was a bloom, a subtle glow about her – *as if someone had lighted a lamp inside her* – Martha thought fancifully as they laughed together at the way in which the life in Dorrit's hair sprang electrically to meet every brush stroke she gave it.

The camp's main mess hall was the scene of the party. The commissariat had excelled itself in the matter of bar supplies and a loaded buffet, and the side attractions included a roulette wheel and an aluminium camel, made in the workshops, acting as a bran tub of absurd, laughter-evoking parcels. There were organized party games and a lottery on the next day's lift of oil. And for once the male world of the camp had a mixture of the other sex – some Italian girls working in Bab Magreb and the French nurses from the hospital there.

Everywhere, in place of the day-to-day "shop" and gossip of the camp, the talk was of the future – of the dazzling potentialities ahead; of the men who, their work done, would be leaving; of the new army of men and machines which would move in – boffins, engineers, oil-riggers, builders; derricks, bulldozers, generators, pipelines; the makings of an airport where there had been a landing-strip; of a city where there was now a mere encampment of lonely pioneers.

Shops, schools, avenues, houses – it had happened elsewhere, in Kuwait, Bahrein, the Sahara, and it would happen here. The air was electric with hope and speculation and plans. But the clamour of talk glanced backwards too, toasting the rigours and the humours of the long, dogged haul which the men who had taken part agreed they would gladly face again for such reward. Or indeed without it, being the stamp of men they were.

As soon as the girls arrived Greg claimed them both and took them to the bar, one hand beneath Dorrit's elbow, his other arm careless on Martha's shoulder. As a gesture it was hardly worth notice, but as always she resented the intimacy which she knew he implied by it. And though, taking her stool, she shrugged clear, as soon as he had ordered for the three of them his palm went between her shoulderblades and stayed there, lightly but possessively.

Jude, along the counter from them, lifted a hand in their direction, then continued talking to his companions. Greg looked, grimaced, then murmured, "And how right I was that Great White Chief Tarleton doesn't love me as a brother! Know what? – the last time he went to Aden I'd been briefed to fly him down. But when he heard that, he asked for Sellars instead, and got him, what's more."

"He was staying over. He probably didn't fancy the kind of night spot a type like you was likely to choose," teased Dorrit.

"That," Greg told her, "is calumny, slander and casting aspersions. Anyway, Sellars didn't wait for him. He came back. And as he had another job on next day, milord had no choice but to put up with me for the return flight or stay put."

"And I suppose you saw that he had a bumpy passage by way of revenge?" asked Dorrit.

"I admit I was sorely tempted. Instead, as he obviously didn't want to talk, I settled for chattering sweet nothings and got under his skin that way." Greg drank quickly and wanted to re-order. But Martha had barely sipped her Martini, and Dorrit, who hadn't touched the gin-and-lime he had insisted she have, asked for a lemonade instead.

"You ought to know by this time, Greg, that I simply can't *like* alcohol, whatever it is," she said.

"Rubbish. You just haven't found your own poison, that's what. I mean, you can't *not* like the stuff in some form or another – it's not natural! For instance, I bet you've never tried – " But though Greg proceeded to list drink after drink by name, Dorrit pursed her lips in distaste at all of them, and at last he gave up.

"You're a freak," he said. "As bad as these Bedouin wallahs. I offered one of them a drink the other day, and you could have said I was withered with a look, no less."

"Well, they don't drink. No orthodox Moslem does. You should know that," said Martha.

"I do now. But my, what they do miss! Or do they, if they're on a built-in pledge since they were born? Rather fun, though" – Greg swirled whisky in his glass reflectively – "to slip one of them a stiff one and then sit back and watch the effect – no?"

"*No!* Though if you're intent on making all of us, as well as yourself, well hated, that would be as good a way as any, I daresay – " At that moment, recognizing one of the nurses she had met at Bab Magreb, Martha made that her excuse for escaping from him and went over to speak to the girl.

There was dancing in a smaller room off the mess hall, and the few girls had only to appear there to be in demand at once. Martha and the French girl spent the next hour there with their partners and then returned with a crowd to sample the buffet. Naomi had appeared once on the dance floor with a slim young Cypriot from one of the seismic teams, and the next time Martha saw her she had joined Jude's group at the bar, commanding all the male attention she usually did.

Later Martha and Dorrit played roulette for a while, then "rode" chairs in a hilarious team race, and both won prizes of nylons at the hoop-la table. By that time it was near the Cinderella hour when Martha and Jude were due to leave. But when she looked round for him he was nowhere in sight, and nor was Dorrit, who had been standing with her, watching the other hoop throwers a few minutes before.

Puzzled that Dorrit should have gone off without saying what she meant to do next, Martha waited, keeping watch for both her and for Jude. At last, deciding she had better fetch her wrap from the cloakroom so that she would be ready to leave when he was, she went there, and in the doorway of the tiny room, met Dorrit, white-faced, strained, and using the doorpost for support until her knees buckled under her and she spread-eagled at Martha's feet.

"Why, Dorrit! Why didn't you – ?" Martha caught back the futile question and knelt, feeling for a pulse and chafing the girl's sweat-beaded cheeks until she opened her eyes. Then Martha reached for the only chair, helped Dorrit into it and with gentle but firm pressure on her nape, thrust her head forward and downward until the restoring blood flowed back to her brain.

She sat up and allowed Martha to smooth her brow and wipe her damp face.

"Where am I? What happened?" she sighed.

"I don't know, except that you've just come round from a faint. Don't you remember feeling ill?" asked Martha.

"I think I do now. Yes – suddenly my head began to swim and I was a lot too hot. I daren't even stop to tell you; I simply ran for it and sat down out here. But I think I must have fallen off the chair, because I found myself on the floor, and I'd just managed to get as far as the door when you say I went off again? Yet I felt so top-of-the-world earlier. So what do you suppose it can be?"

Martha said again, "I don't know. It could be the heat in the hall. Or something you've eaten, perhaps. But I'm going to bring Jude to have a look at you, and we'll take you home with us."

But to Martha's dismay Jude was still not in evidence when she returned to the hall. The first man she asked thought he had already left. The next contradicted this, claiming he was still around. It was Nick Murray who suggested he might be waiting for Martha in his car, and though, as they had arranged to meet at the bar, she thought this unlikely, she agreed to go and see, leaving Nick to look for Jude in the men's room.

At first she despaired of finding Jude's car quickly among the jeeps, the land-rovers and the huge covered tonneaux which had brought the men in to the party from the camps and which now packed the tarmac, nose to tail. But as she skirted the perimeter fence she believed she saw the car ahead, parked half in, half out of the immediate darkness beyond an arc-light pylon.

Yes, it was there, and Jude must be too, for she could just discern silhouetted movement at its near side. She quickened her steps to a run, and then, within yards, herself in the shadow of a jeep, suddenly froze in her tracks and turned . . . straight into the unyielding bulk of Nick Murray's chest and the arms he put out to check her blind rush from what she had seen.

Nick began, "Hey – whoa there!" and stopped, looking beyond and behind her as he steadied her, then released her.

"Oh," he said. "I see. Dicey, that – Do you really want Jude badly enough to interrupt?"

Martha said urgently, "Yes . . . yes, he must come. To Dorrit. She's been taken ill – "

Nick said, peering, "That's Naomi with him. All right. If you like to cut back to Dorrit, I'll manage to trip over something between here and there and make the welkin ring with my curses, which should give 'em time to unlock."

"Thanks, Nick. You agree they mustn't guess that I, that we – ?"

He grinned. "Well, naturally. Otherwise, red faces all round. You can trust me. Oh, before you go, where is Jude to find you when he comes back?"

She told him, then ran, even her hurry for Dorrit's sake now overlaid by her own need to escape without being tempted to a backward glance at the two in the shadows, straining together in a passion which once, on another night of warm, seductive darkness, Jude's male impulse had felt briefly for her.

For her then. For Naomi tonight. Tomorrow – for whom?

CHAPTER IX

The next day, when Martha returned from visiting Dorrit, Naomi's luggage stood in the porch, awaiting the car which was to take her to the airstrip. Naomi, still in her room making a check of the contents of her dressing-case, called out when she heard Martha come in.

"Well, keep me posted," Naomi invited. "How is the Little Mother-To-Be? Is she? Or isn't she? Or doesn't anyone know?"

Martha went to stand in the doorway, noting the room's stripped emptiness and wondering how much or how little Naomi regretted the closing of this chapter of her life. She said, "Dorrit? She is, Jude is pretty sure, and doesn't think her faint last night is much to worry about. But she has got to rest until her tests come through."

"And I suppose she and Ben are coming over all conventionally pleased?"

"They're ecstatic," said Martha bluntly. "You'd think they'd invented the whole idea of babies. But is there anything odd about that?"

"Not a thing. It's quite usual, I believe. And if that's the way they want it, they're welcome – " As Naomi spoke she snapped down the clasps of her case and allowed Martha to take it from her while she threw a last glance round the room, then came out, shutting the door on it for the last time.

In the living room she offered cigarettes and they made

the brittle conversation of people waiting for a train to pull out, an air flight to be called, a ship's siren to blow. Martha asked what time Naomi hoped to reach Aden, which pilot she would have and whether Ben or Jude were seeing her off.

Naomi said, "I don't think so. I've blotted my copy-book with Ben; he doesn't mince his opinion that I'm letting the side down by leaving. And as Jude and I took our leave of each other last night, it might smack of anti-climax to stage our grand finale all over again, don't you think?"

"Don't . . . *I* think?"

"Well, you were there, in a stalls seat, weren't you?"

"You mean – on the tarmac? You – saw me?"

Naomi nodded. "I did. Jude didn't. I was facing your way, and let's say he was rather absorbed in his work. But if you stayed long enough, I dare say you see what I mean about his – technique?"

Martha stirred uncomfortably. "But if you know he means nothing lasting or sincere by it, why – ?"

"Why do I co-operate?" Naomi paused, watching the smoke of her cigarette. "Because, I suppose, I come in much the same mould myself. Jude kisses and rides smartly back to the real love of his life – his work; I kiss and move on to the next man who amuses me or, better still, who would like to ignore me but can't. There are soldiers of fortune in our sex too, you know, and I happen to be one of them."

"But don't you ever want the real thing? Haven't you ever been in love?"

"I don't think so. I go through the motions, but it doesn't last. The sixty-four-dollar question is whether or not I could spend the rest of my life with the current man, and up to date the answer has always been no. And even if I do shop around as much as a man does without anyone thinking the worse of him until he's actually committed, at least I play it straight. If I suspect it's getting too serious, I've my own methods of moving out and on – fast."

"And doesn't it matter to you that sometimes you must hurt women?"

"I never do – when I know there's one in the background. Besides, a man who is fighting his conscience tends to make much more heavy weather of an affair than it's worth to me. No, I prefer 'em footloose and fancy-free."

"But won't you find, as you get older yourself, that the type who can attract you isn't going to be either?"

"That's what's known as an occupational risk. When it begins to happen too often, at best I can always take up good works, and at worst, I can get me to a nunnery. Meanwhile, it suits me to walk alone and set to whatever partners I choose as I go – " Naomi stood, smoothing her skirt and touching her piled hair. "Here's my car," she said. "Zero hour."

But somehow, in the moment of parting, Martha suddenly saw her for the infinitely lonely figure she was. She followed her out to the car, and when Naomi, her cases loaded, held out her hand with a cool, "Well – ?" Martha said impulsively, "No, not yet, please. I'll see you off, if I may."

Naomi shrugged and withdrew her hand. "Do," she said indifferently, and made room beside her.

At the landing-strip Martha was glad of the impulse which had brought her. For the male attention Naomi could always command in off-duty hours was non-existent for her in the workaday world of the camp where at this hour there were very few men about, except for a couple of mechanics busy on the waiting plane. David Sellars came out to make his last checks and embraced

Naomi expansively. Then he was ready to take off, and with the need for goodbyes really upon them Martha found nothing less trite with which to speed Naomi into her future than, "Well, good luck. You won't lose touch? You'll let us know how you get on, where you go?"

Naomi smiled thinly. "Out of sight, out of mind. A month, and not one of you could care less." She paused, then to Martha's surprise, bent to kiss her lightly on the cheek. "Meanwhile, don't waste your time," she advised.

"Waste my time? What do you mean? What in?" Martha asked.

"In caring for Jude. Because there's no future in it," said Naomi, and stepped up into the tiny cabin without looking back.

Overnight, when Jude had asked her to wait within call while he examined Dorrit, Martha's intuition had realized the probable cause both of the girl's earlier air of radiance and of the fainting attack which had seemed to belie it, and Jude's snap diagnosis had confirmed her guess.

He had told Martha so on his way to fetch the car for the three of them, and when she had rejoined Dorrit she had found her starry-eyed – there was no other word for it – with wonder at the prospect before her.

"He says he's almost sure I'm going to have a baby," she had announced.

"And you needed Jude to tell you! Hadn't you suspected you might be going to, yourself?" Martha teased her.

"Well, I'd sort of hoped – But when I felt so ill just now I was frightened. Just imagine it, Martha – a baby of my own! Not someone else's, that I have to give back or say goodbye to – *mine*!"

"Here, steady on! It'll be half Ben's too, you know!"

Dorrit had sighed happily. "Yes, of course – ours," she said, making the monosyllable the symbol of fulfilment which it was.

But though, after the precautionary week's rest which Jude prescribed for her, she continued to help in the clinic and on the wards, it was not long before she and Ben had to face the changes which the coming of the baby would demand of their lives. As Ben put it ruefully, they had jumped the gun too soon. In its now secure and foreseeable future Taroued would be a place where European babies could be born and reared and educated and married off by the hundred. But nine months hence it could still be little more than the stark outpost of the desert it was now, with no room in it for any baby who could and should be born elsewhere.

That meant England and the closing of the Taroued chapter in Ben's career, as Naomi's had already closed for her. But he planned to stay on until Jude had engaged his successor in the lab, and even longer if the summer humidity did not prove too much for Dorrit.

Meanwhile a new laboratory assistant was due in Naomi's place and already the hospital had tasted modest affluence in the shape of a new ambulance. There was extra unskilled help to come; later, more nurses, new equipment, at least a third doctor or surgeon, ambitious building plans.

Endings and beginnings . . . Sometimes, in the despairs of the small hours which come to everyone, Martha wondered how many of the latter she would be there to see; how long she could bear to work with Jude, for him, because of him, with the memory of one night in his arms to tantalize and shame her with its falseness, its cheapness, and without hope that his everyday need of her and dependence on her work promised anything she craved of him . . . anything at all.

It had been Naomi who had proved and underlined that there were two Jude Tarletons. One, the "very ordinary man" with passing needs and impulses which he despised; the other, dedicated and undeviating from the purpose he had set himself. And neither of them for any woman with pride of her own or with a love for him that asked some return.

So, she thought, when the time came and she was free to go, she might do just that, against all her aching longing to stay to see Taroued fulfilled and Jude's work with it. Another flight from love to be lived down . . . lived through. Another ending for her before other people's beginnings had happened in earnest, she told herself in dreary self-pity, without the foreknowledge then of how a few careless words she had already forgotten speaking were to precipitate someone else's "ending" first.

One morning, at the end of the clinic session, she was alone there, ready to lock up and go off duty when a jeep stopped in the forecourt and Greg appeared at the door.

"Knock, knock. Shop still open?" he asked.

"Only just," she told him. "What can it do for you?"

He showed his hand, carelessly bandaged. "Just a knife cut. Nothing to write home about."

Nor was it. It was a long gash, not deep, across the ball of his thumb. It had not bled much, and Martha was surprised he should have brought it to the clinic for attention.

As she fetched dressing and bandage for it, "Can't you get first aid at the camp for this kind of thing?" she asked, knowing that he could if he had troubled to do so.

"Of course. But I thought it would be cosier to make you my ministering angel. Any objections?"

"None," she said coolly. "It's what I'm here for –

when I'm here. But as I mightn't have been on duty this morning was your journey really necessary?"

"Opportunity being a fine thing, yes. Because I suppose you realize I have to make my own chances of seeing you these days and risk a brush-off when I do?"

She finished his bandage and collected her kit. "You know why," she said.

He smiled, none too agreeably. "But naturally I know why! You've decided I need slapping down for having jilted you, and playing hard-to-get is your way of doing it –"

At that she rounded on him. "I've done nothing of the sort!" she denied.

"Then what – ?" he invited.

"Ought you to need telling *again*? I've avoided you because we're finished. I – I've grown out of you. I had to run away from you to here. But it worked, and now we've nothing to say to each other any more."

"Haven't we?" Greg's brows went up. "If I thought you meant that, my ego might be quite crushed. But d'you know, I really doubt if you do?"

"I don't know why you should think I don't, since it's the truth!"

He shook his head. "Not it. You're over-playing, that's all. Because if it wasn't going to do something for you to have me around, why didn't you give the thumbs-down signal when you had the chance?"

Martha stared at him, too surprised to pretend ignorance of his meaning. "How do you know I was offered any say in whether you stayed or went?" she asked.

From his flash of expression she saw that he hadn't known; he had merely ventured a long shot which had gone home. Admitting it, he said, "Just a guess. You see, I figured someone was likely to sound you unofficially on your reactions to your 'ex' being offered Will

Shorthouse's job, and it seems I was right. Who was it, by the way? Dumont, or Tarleton direct? Or did they employ a go-between?"

"It was Jude."

"Well, well! He said, 'Does he' – meaning me – 'get the push or not?' And you said, 'Let him stay' – because it suited you to have me dangling while you marked time over when, where and how you would kiss and make it up – "

"I did *not*! It was simply that I hadn't the right to decide such a thing either way, and I told Jude so."

Greg affected awe. "And there's finesse! 'She didn't say yes, she didn't say no' – knowing, the little hedge-sitter, that I'd be staying if she didn't weigh in against me! And it worked. You got what you wanted – me, to keep at arm's length until you judged the time was ripe for me to be forgiven. But don't I get a break soon? For instance, do you realize I haven't kissed you once since that first boss-shot after I crashed?"

Martha said, "That was a failure because I meant it to be, and my feelings haven't changed since then."

"Come to that, nor have mine!" he flashed.

Suddenly she felt helpless in face of his obtuse refusal to take his dismissal. "Oh, Greg," she appealed, "what's the use of going on like this? For the last time – I don't love you any longer and I don't want you to think I ever shall again. But if only you can be generous enough to accept that, is there any reason in the world why we shouldn't still be friends?"

He came closer and stood over her. "Friends!" he spat. "Just how corny can you get? As if any man in his right senses ever made a friend of a *woman* – " Then his hands went to her shoulders, crushing her to him, and his lips took hers in a deliberate, enforced kiss of which he made an even greater insult than his words.

"Greg, let me go!"

"How badly do you really want me to?" he taunted her.

"You should know – " Suddenly, as he laughed without humour at her struggles to free herself, her anger flamed. She stilled then, deceptively, and as soon as his imprisoning hold relaxed she wrenched a hand free and slapped him full across the cheek.

She saw tears of shock start into his eyes and she was glad, fiercely glad. He exploded, "Why, you little – !" ready with an ugliness which went unspoken as Ahmadi put his head round the door and spoke to Martha.

"I have taken the drug basket. I go now, *Tabiba* Shore?"

"Yes, that's all, Ahmadi. I'm just off myself."

"Hold hard a minute. Going my way?" That was Greg, his back turned to Martha, addressing the young Arab.

Ahmadi, surprised, looked from one to the other. "I go home," he said.

"Well, that's all right. Show me where, and I'll drop you," Greg offered. Then, without a backward glance at Martha, he strode out, Ahmadi at his heels, and a minute or two later she heard the churning of the jeep's engine before it drove away.

For hours after that she tried to recall the person she must have been so short a while ago; the one who had loved Greg so blindly as never to have faced his nastier side, when his will was crossed. Their engagement couldn't have been all idyllic agreement; they must have quarrelled sometimes. Had she always then given in just short of the flashpoint which would have shown his ugly streak for what it was? She supposed she must have done, warned by the instinct which knew it was there, but wanted it kept out of sight and out of mind in the name of love.

And what now? Now, she suspected, his malice might not stop at mere avoidance of her. She could not foresee any way in which he could harm her. But he would if he could. Of that she felt sure.

She returned to the hospital in the late afternoon and, since there was to be no evening clinic, she was surprised to see two Bedouin women waiting in the forecourt. Nearer, she recognized them both. The slight one, Mina; the stout, older woman, her mother-in-law, without whom or some other escort Mina did not now go out.

Martha hurried to them. "Mina, how good to see you! And Madame Mounia bint Haradj – Come in, won't you, and Jahra shall make coffee. Or" – she broke off at sight of Mina's troubled eyes -- "is anything the matter? Something I can help with? Tell me."

The older woman's only response was a forlorn weaving of her head, but Mina said breathlessly, "It is Ahmadi, *tabiba*. He has not come home to his house. Since morning he has not come, and I worry. His mother also troubles herself. For he has no habit of lingering in the markets as other men have, and today he should have slept, to be ready to return for his duty of the night hours after he had been to the mosque for the evening prayers. So we come to see if it happens that you know where – ?"

"– where he can be?" Martha shook her head in perplexity. "No. He left here as always. Oh – " She bit her lip as she remembered how and with whom Ahmadi had gone. "That is, he went in a car with one of the air pilots from the camp who had come for some treatment to his hand. But Ahmadi meant to come home. He said so."

"Yet he comes not. Evil has befallen him. *Inshallah*," mourned his mother in Arabic.

Martha said gently, "We must hope not. But you did

155

right to come here. If there has been an accident the hospital will have heard of it."

As she spoke she shepherded them into the clinic and left them there while she went to make inquiries of the staff who had been on duty during the day. To her relief there had been no call to an accident, but equally no one could suggest what might have happened to Ahmadi since he had left the clinic with Greg. She decided her next move must be a radio call to the camp to contact Greg, and she was on her way to put this through when she passed two giggling boy orderlies on their way to the wards, and checked as her ear caught Ahmadi's name.

"Hassan! Mohammet!" she broke into their chatter. "You speak of Ahmadi. Where is he?" And then, when the boys' only reply was a sheepish giggle and a shuffling of their feet, "Come," she urged sharply, "if you have seen him or know where he is now, tell me."

More giggles, exasperating though reassuring in their way, she supposed. Then Hassan ventured, "We do not know where he is now, *tabiba*. But we have seen him. In the markets. With a *Nazarani* who goes – *so*."

A Christian with a limp. Hassan's mimicry of the slight remaining stiffness of Greg's injured leg was graphic. Martha nodded. "Yes, I know the *Nazarani*. And he and Ahmadi were together in the markets – when?"

Some argument ensued as to when before it emerged that it had been an hour or two earlier and that Greg and Ahmadi were not on their way through but making, as it were, a day of it.

Martha mentioned the jeep. "They were in a working motor-car?"

They had a "rough" car, yes, Mohammet admitted. But they were afoot when the boys had seen them. They were going from booth to booth making fun with some traders, angering others. For they were – Mohammet sought a word, then, embarrassed, substituted action. "They were . . . thus, *tabiba*," he said, his lolling head and rocking, wide-legged stance description enough.

Drunk? Martha said sharply, "How could this be? Ahmadi is a good Moslem. He does not drink!"

Mohammet shrugged and looked at Hassan for support. "We have seen it, *tabiba*. We know it was so," he insisted.

Drunk! Both of them! Martha's anger against Greg was a whiplash she would have liked to use on him. How dared he? How *dared* he? she raged inwardly. For she was in no doubt that this – his incitement of Ahmadi to a vice quite foreign to him – was his retort direct to her rejection of him, one mean way of hitting back at her while he plotted others. Oh yes, he had turned enemy all right, and for a start he could not have found a better way than this of bringing the hospital into disrepute with the people it served.

And it was she, she realized, who had given him the clue when he had suggested it might be "fun", and she had warned him roundly of the consequences, never guessing then how evilly he would make use of the knowledge.

She told Mohammet, "Very well. If you say you saw it, I believe you," then sent both boys on their way. But what to do now? She abandoned the idea of radioing the camp, since it was unlikely Greg would either take Ahmadi there or return himself until he was sober. The evening market would not yet be open, so they would not still be there. Therefore the best hope was that they had parted company and that Ahmadi at least had made his way home by now.

For a minute or two she stood in thought, and was about to go back to Mina with a toned-down version of the story and the advice to wait for Ahmadi at home if

157

he was not already there when a door from the forecourt opened and Jude strode in, his face set and his hand in a police-grip under the elbow of the shambling figure beside him . . . Ahmadi. An Ahmadi who, she realized with a stab of relief, was already almost sobered by some sharp experience nearer in time than his orgy with Greg.

At sight of him she breathed, "Oh, thank goodness! Where did you find him?" she asked Jude.

"At Base, where I'd gone to see a patient," he said shortly.

"At the *camp*? Then Greg did – "

"Greg? So you're in the picture?" Jude put in.

"Partly. When I came back on duty Mina and her mother-in-law were waiting for me, worried to death that Ahmadi hadn't been home, and I knew he had left here with Greg this morning."

"Just a minute. I'm not with you. I'd supposed they had met somewhere in the town. What was Ryder doing here this morning?"

"After you had gone on your rounds and just before I was ready to close the clinic he came with a cut hand to be dressed, and he offered Ahmadi a lift home."

"And that's all you know?"

"No. I've just heard from Hassan and Mohammet that there was some kind of drunken scene in the markets later." Martha added quickly, "But you can't blame Ahmadi for that."

"I don't. You haven't heard the rest?"

"What – rest?"

Jude ignored the question and answered his own. "No, of course there hasn't been time. Well, here it is. After they left the markets, which wasn't, I gather, until they were more or less drummed out, Ryder took Ahmadi over to Base, proposing to give him not only his first trip by air, but his first lesson at the controls of a plane."

Martha stared, aghast. "But the boys said Greg was drunk too!"

"Exactly." Jude's tone was grim. "Otherwise let's hope even he could hardly be such a criminal fool."

"But he was stopped?"

"Not until he had smuggled Ahmadi into the cockpit and they were on the point of taking off. Then a mechanic gave the alarm and they were hauled out by Dumont in person."

"If they'd crashed the plane they might have killed themselves!" breathed Martha.

"If they'd crashed the plane they might have killed other people, which would have been worse. As it was, sheer fright had pretty well sobered up our friend here by the time I arrived on the scene, and I left Dumont spoiling to deal with Ryder without benefit of gloves – " Jude paused and surveyed Ahmadi with a measuring eye. "As for you, we'll settle accounts later. Meanwhile, you'd better get home and sleep it off."

None too steadily Ahmadi stood his ground. "It will not be so again with me, *Tabib* Tarleton. You know that of me?" he pleaded.

"I hope I do. I think so. Now be off with you and report to me in the morning. Eight o'clock sharp in my office, d'you hear?"

Ahmadi drew himself up. "I have no time for sleep, *tabib*. I am on night duty after sunset."

Not without irony Jude said, "It does you credit to remember as much, but we'll manage without you, I dare say." Turning to Martha, he asked, "Are Mina and his mother still here?" and when she told him, "Yes, in the clinic," his gesture in that direction brooked no more lingering on Ahmadi's part.

When he had gone, "Let's hope Mina will relieve her

feelings by giving him the curtain lecture he deserves," Jude said. And then, "As for Ryder, Martha, I'm afraid you've got to face it that this means he's finished here. Smuggling an unauthorized person on to the landing-ground, drunk at the controls of an aircraft, needing manhandling to get him out of the cockpit – neither Dumont nor the Company are going to wear it, you know."

Martha said, "You can't think I'd want them to? But I hate even more what he did to Ahmadi. That was un-forgivable – to use him and Mina's worry for him as a weapon against me – "

"Against you? Do you mean you and he had quarrelled and you're suggesting he took Ahmadi off on a drunken jag out of pique?"

"It was more than pique. It was deliberate malice he knew I should understand, because I had told him about the contempt the Bedouins have for drink and for anyone who tempts them to it."

"But in this case that was Ryder himself, surely?"

"Not only Greg. You know they might not distinguish between him and the rest of us in the matter of blame!"

Jude shook his head. "I know what you mean – mud spreads and sticks. But I think you needn't worry too much – we're beginning to be well enough thought of to be able to ride it now. So you did quarrel with Ryder this morning?"

"It was more than a quarrel. I made him my enemy for good. He had persuaded himself that I had had the say-so about his getting his job, and he seemed to think that gave him rights over me that he hasn't had since he broke our engagement."

Jude regarded her thoughtfully. "But could you claim, hand on heart, that you haven't yourself to blame for that? You haven't noticeably kept him at arm's length, have you?"

"It wasn't easy. He knew I still loved him when he broke with me, and he always refused to accept that we couldn't pick up the threads again, just like that."

"Yet you wouldn't say the one word to me which would have sent him on his way?"

"He had no job to go to, and he had forfeited his right to a reference from D.L.C. He's a good pilot and Monsieur Dumont needed him. How could I have said, 'Yes, get rid of him, please, because he's an embarrassment to me'? It wouldn't have been fair!"

"You still needn't have handed me the half-truth you did – that I had no right to thrust the decision on to you. Anyway, I doubt whether you could have been as fair as all that if you were never in two minds about forgiving him and taking him back as soon as you were free of your contract here."

"I never was. You've *got* to believe I didn't want him to stay!"

"Yet I merited so little of your confidence that until now you wouldn't admit as much and leave the rest to me? All right, at least you convince me you've finally taken his measure now, and I'm glad. But you know, Martha" – the corner of Jude's mouth lifted as if in wry despair of her – "when you choose to dig in your heels on a matter of principle, as you did in our clash over Nura's rescue and again over Ryder, you do try goodwill and sympathy rather far. Not to mention a friendship which you must know is yours for the asking – And you do, don't you? Because surely, professional dependence on each other apart, we've the makings of friendship by now?"

Friendship? Ah yes, if that was all he had to offer her, or wanted of her, it had to be enough. Better the half-loaf than no bread until you outlived hunger or came to terms with it . . . And so, "Friends? Why, yes, I've always hoped we could be that," she said, then left him, shrinking from meeting mere cordiality in his eyes while all her heart was in her own.

CHAPTER X

Two days later Greg had gone. By the camp manager's orders he remained a virtual prisoner in his quarters before he left, and he took leave of no one but his housemate and David Sellars, who flew him down to Aden. On the return flight David brought back a pilot to replace him, and the self-contained world of the camp, busy with its glowing future, promptly forgot him.

Nor did his drunken escapade have the repercussions he had intended. But it was Jude who was to be thanked for that, Martha knew. At his suggestion, he and Monsieur Dumont devoted a day to assessing the annoyance and damage which Greg and Ahmadi had caused in the markets. Compensation was paid, suspicion and ill-feeling dispersed, and the story passed without rancour into the gossip of the old men over their hookahs and the chatter of the women at the wells.

Meanwhile the small community, lacking all food resource but its domestic livestock and the meagre crops it tended and harvested on tiny holdings snatched from the desert, faced its yearly threat of near-famine between the end of winter and the time of the spring sowings.

The consequences came to the clinic in the shape of wailing babies, toddlers on matchstick legs and mothers who made bread and rationed milk for the children without allotting a share for themselves. Morning after morning Martha stood by while Jude or Ben advised and prescribed for malnutrition, and she was always loud

163

with protest afterwards.

"Isn't it *anyone's* responsibility to see that they feed all the year round and not just while their own produce lasts?" she clamoured to Jude.

He looked up from his desk. "We're working on it," he said. "Don't forget they are a nomad race, used to eating what they've got while it's there and moving on when it's not. Things are changing. This lot have settled here and they'll stay, and ultimately they won't want for much. But the habits of centuries die hard, and you can't expect them to go all community-minded and see the virtues of a rationing system overnight."

"Then you are trying to introduce one?" Martha persisted.

"Under the Sheikh's distinguished patronage, yes. There's a scheme afoot by which every settlement in the territory is supposed to declare the size of its wheat or millet harvest and its requirements for food and seed, with the surplus going for distribution. But you can't budget for much surplus after a season of poor rains like last summer; you've got to reckon that figures of yields are going to be 'cooked' and that here, for instance, you're up against a handful of spivs who bought or bartered cheap and are sitting on stocks, planning to sell dear on the black market."

"Do you know that's happening?"

"We suspect it without the means of proving it, and the three or four characters I have in view don't appear to have a bushel of grain or a side of goat's meat too many on their premises." Jude rose, and as he passed Martha on his way out his hand rested momentarily on her shoulder.

"I warned you, remember, that Arabia had its sinister faces? Well, this is one of them, and the remedy is long-term. But it'll come all right, and making sure that it does is what we're here for, isn't it?"

But the promise of plenty for Taroued when the desert flowered at the dictates of the oilmen did little for Martha's compassion for people who were hungry now. She envied Jude his authority which could badger the Government, the Sheikh, more productive settlements and the Company for funds. At least he could act, *do* something about it. Whereas for her there was only pity and impatience and a futile sense of guilt whenever she ate well herself.

More and more Ben was deputizing for Jude when he was out and about in connection with the problem. And he was in Bab Magreb, summoned by the Sheikh, on an afternoon when Martha, who had walked to a visit of her own, had returned to the hospital too early for the evening clinic but without its being worthwhile to go back to her quarters for the hour she had to spare. There was always a backlog of clerical work, entering up the patients' record cards, and she was busy with this when the door opened and a Bedouin whose face she remembered came in.

He bowed. "*Salaam aleikum, ó tabiba.* Is the *Tabib* Tarleton here?" he asked.

Martha smiled. He was Youssif, whose wife's baby they had delivered on her own first night in Taroued. She returned his greeting in Arabic, adding that though Jude was not available, Ben would be there for the evening clinic after his return from his rounds.

Youssif shook his head. "That will be too late."

"Too late?"

Martha's heart had missed a beat, but Youssif's explanation was reassuring. It was his good "house", he said, who had had the thought and now insisted that the doctor must see the baby before they left on their journey. There was nothing amiss with the baby. But

165

Fatima would have it so – the *tabiba* understood?

Martha agreed that she did. Mothers were like that, she said. "When are you going on your journey, Youssif, and how far?" she added.

"To the Outer Tents, where they have hunted ibex and so have meat to share and where there is still grain for making bread. We travel in the cool of the evening and night, and we should have gone at dawn if Fatima had not had this thought about the baby," Youssif said.

Martha said, "Very soon now – the *Tabib* Tarleton is seeing to it – there should be meat and meal for you here. So must you take this journey?"

But as she put the question she realized she was arguing against the nomad instinct of which Jude had spoken – the urge to go in search of food when supplies failed on the spot. And Youssif's reply confirmed this.

"When there is meat in Taroued we shall return. But now we must go without the *tabib* seeing the baby?"

"If you must leave by this sunset, yes. But I will come and look at the baby, if that will make Fatima content to go?"

Youssif beamed. If the *tabiba* would do that, Allah would grant that the whole world should love her, he declared. And she would come with him now?

"Yes, now," said Martha, and they set out, Youssif conducting her by a shorter cut than the car had taken that first night or on her later visits to Fatima with Jude or Dorrit. When they reached the three-sided courtyard of which Youssif's house formed the narrow back end, it was clear that he intended that the family's trek should begin as soon as Martha had pronounced on the baby's fitness for it. For his mule – Fatima's transport – stood waiting, heavily panniered; no hens now pecked or rustled about the open ground floor, and Youssif would have called to Fatima to bring the baby down if Martha had not said she preferred to examine him upstairs.

Fatima too was veiled and ready with yet more gear to be loaded on to the long-suffering mule, while Youssif Junior, whom Fatima was still feeding herself, appeared to be in much bonnier shape than Martha had hoped to find him. Yes, he could travel with safety, she took the responsibility of telling Fatima. And when he was swaddled and be-capped and was wearing the right talisman for the journey, Fatima looked about her, said, "Then now all is arranged," and with quiet dignity led the way out and down the stairs.

At sight of the extra luggage Youssif protested in the best male tradition that it could not go, it should not go, and did Fatima suppose that their friends of the Outer Tents could not provide them with a *buchari* for their tea? But he set to work to rearrange the load, and while he did so Martha looked up at the silent windowless first floors on either side of the courtyard.

"You have no neighbours, Youssif?" she asked.

He looked up, following her glance. "No one, *tabiba*. But these are not dwellings. This one" – he jerked a thumb – "is a store place for camel trappings, millstones, other things. That, a granary."

"A granary? You keep your own grain there when you have some?"

"I have to buy my flour. I am a camel-driver," he reminded her. "No, Hadrassi the merchant hires the place from me for too little silver. But it is empty now. Hadrassi, like his fellows, will have no more wheat to store or sell until harvest." Youssif tightened a girth, helped Fatima to mount, took the mule by the bridle and was ready to go.

Martha waved them goodbye and was about to leave herself when a solitary hen padded into the courtyard from the street and began to scratch in the dust beneath

167

the harness place.

She watched it idly. It must be a stray from a neighbouring yard; Fatima had said all Youssif's flock had long since gone for the pot. "Better find your way home. Nothing there for you, hen," Martha addressed it. But in the way of hens it ignored the human voice, changed course to cross to the other side, where it began to pick so busily that Martha felt curious to see what it was getting.

She followed it into the shadow of the overhang of the upper floor. It was semi-dark there and she had to stoop to see what the hen had found. It was corn . . . wheat, dropping in a thin, small rain from a knothole overhead and forming a pile of grains faster than the hen could peck.

Martha stared, fascinated, expecting the trickle to stop at any moment. But it came on, its flow seemingly limited only by the size of the knothole outlet, until even the hen was replete and strolled away, leaving Martha alone with the puzzle of grain flowing without stint from a granary where no grain was supposed to be.

She frowned, catching at a memory. *Hadrassi* – ! She remembered now that though the names had meant little to her, at one time Jude had mentioned those of the few black market suspects, and Hadrassi had been one of them. Hadrassi, like the other merchants, had no stocks on his premises, nothing to sell for his own profit, nothing surplus for requisition. But Hadrassi found it worth his while to rent storage space from Youssif for non-existent grain – *why?*

Pondering, Martha looked at the palmful she held. It was real enough and it was still dropping. More where it came from? If so, how had Youssif not known it was there, waiting until it could be sold in secret at an outrageous price? *Or had he known* and had lied to her? That

168

she hated to believe. But money, bribery to a poor man to hold his tongue could explain it. Could explain too Youssif's flitting. Suppose he had moved out to avoid the backwash of trouble and exposure for Hadrassi if there were any to come?

Well, there was going to be in plenty if – Martha flung down the wheat in her hand and scanned the blackened underside of the flooring above her head. From the ground to Youssif's first floor there was a stairway. Here there was none. But there was something else – the outline of a close-fitting trapdoor, just discernible by the flange along one side against which a ladder might rest.

There was no ladder. Frustrated and bent now on trespass, Martha stared up at the square of the trapdoor until her eyes ached. Then she remembered that she had noticed a ladder lying along the back wall of Youssif's ground floor. It might be too heavy for her to lift or drag; it could prove too short to reach the flange of the trapdoor, which latter would almost certainly be locked. Three chances against her, none in her favour. But she went in search of the ladder all the same.

It was reasonably light and it was long enough for the purpose. An impediment to her short climb was the shoulder-satchel containing her treatment kit, but she slung this diagonally so that it bobbed on her back, and went up.

To her surprise there was neither lock nor bolt to the trapdoor. Fast only by the closeness of its fit, it gave heavily and slowly when she braced herself on the ladder and pressed up on it with both hands, and though something prevented it from falling full back, when it stood at right angles to the aperture and seemed firm, she took another step up the ladder and pulled herself over the edge.

She straightened, accustoming her eyes to the twilight

of the long room, noticing first the obstacle to the trap-door – a laden sack, lurching sideways of its own weight on its base – then other sacks, piled in places to roof level, some spilling their contents from ragged holes, and finally the sea of loose wheat about the floor.

So – ! Her long shot of deduction had paid off – Hadrassi's mean, illicit hoard was here by the bushel, the hundredweight, the ton, enough to feed hungry children with bread for many a long day. But how had he amassed it and off-loaded it in secret? And how, the ugly thought stabbed again, could Youssif not have known?

Martha glanced at her watch. Time had passed too quickly, and now she had little enough to spare to get back for Ben's clinic and to tell her news. But first, on the notion of discovering how that knothole had rained the continuous stream it had, she moved about the floor, scuffing grain aside with her feet, and found it quickly, about where she judged it to be.

Now the flow had stopped. Its "feed" – a hole in a sack slumped on its side – had no more to give. But there were more holes, small ones, their edges ragged, bitten, the surface around them befouled . . . . *Rats!* On her sick recoil of distaste Martha turned quickly back to the trapdoor – just as the sagging bulk of its prop canted away from it, leaving it to teeter on its hinges for a split second, the chances even as to its falling back or forward into place.

It fell forward with a crash. But though Martha's taut nerves jumped at the noise, she had no misgivings about lifting it until she knelt to do so. Then she saw it had neither ring nor crosspiece to act as handhold and that it fitted – or had jammed – so flush that it gave not even a knifeblade's play of space by which it might be prised open.

At first she refused to accept its defiance, and raided her kit for her only available tool – surgical scissors. But neither they nor the scrabble of her fingernails would serve, and as she sat back on her heels, acknowledging defeat, for the first time in her life she understood what it was to feel her scalp crawl with fear. Sweat beaded coldly on her upper lip and her eyelids, and it took a conscious effort of will to get a grip on herself, to look her fear in the face and try to cut it down to size.

It was, she knew, as much a fear of sharing her prison with the rats when the swift, full dark came down as it was her dread of discovery by Hadrassi before she was missed elsewhere.

And how soon or late might that be? She wrenched her thoughts from the rats to work it out.

She had left a message for Ben, saying where she had gone. But he might not worry nor, even if he did, be free to look into her absence until the end of his clinic, which could well last until dark. That meant, at best, over an hour more; at worst, that when Ben sent or came in search of her, he would find Youssif's house empty and Youssif gone, and unless he read aright the clue of the ladder below, what was there to tell him where she was?

Only a blank wall faced the yard; there was not even a slit from which she could fly a signal. On the thin hope of a door giving through into Youssif's first floor, she went to that end of the loft – finding a door, certainly, but one that was locked fast. She realized the futility of beating on the thick outer wall, and though she could shout, what hope was there that she could time even that to the chance of being heard?

For all that, she tried – only to be mocked by the answering silence. None of Youssif's neighbours lived near enough to hear. Hadrassi – No, she would *not* contemplate the possibility of his coming before Ben did! She would shout again at intervals and must hope she would hear Ben come into the yard. Meanwhile she could only wait.

One more fruitless assault on the trapdoor, then she lugged some sacks into the rough shape of a throne on which she perched, well clear of the floor which, after dark, would be sinister with comings and goings. If only she had a torch! If only – glancing at the ingrained filth of her hands and guessing that her face was no cleaner – she hadn't lost her handkerchief!

But search revealed that indeed she had, and as she made do with a square of surgical gauze from her kitbag, somehow the possession of both a torch and a handkerchief looked like the proverbial riches which surpassed the dreams of avarice.

Already there were rustlings among the wheat and she sensed the bright, wary eyes which watched her. She shouted and heard her voice crack, go out of control. This was the edge of panic, she knew. "Oh, please, Ben, hurry!" she prayed. Jude – ? But Jude, about Taroued's business in Bab Magreb, seemed very far away.

Jude said curtly, "Let's get this straight, may we? You first missed her – when?"

Watched anxiously by Dorrit, Ben took a quarterdeck march the length of his living room. "Look, Chief, I've told you already how it went!" he protested.

"Then tell me again. Only make it snappy."

"Well, there was this note she left for me. You've seen it yourself – "

"Yes, yes – saying she had gone to look at Youssif's baby before clinic time. And you took the clinic alone, without feeling over-concerned as to why she hadn't shown up?"

Ben appealed again, "Look, Chief, that's not fair.

How was I to know what might have delayed her? Anything could have. Besides, the world and his wife – *all* his wives – turned up at the clinic tonight. But when Martha hadn't arrived by the end of it, I sent Ahmadi to scout for her and myself hared back to her quarters and here, to see if she had skipped the clinic for some reason. Because she was ill or something – "

"And Ahmadi's story is that he found neither Youssif nor Fatima to question; the house was shut up and the neighbours he asked told him that Youssif had taken his wife and baby off to the Outer Tents at dawn? But that makes nonsense of Martha's note to you. D'you suppose Ahmadi is telling the truth? *Did* he go to the house? Or question anyone?"

At that Dorrit broke in, "Oh, Jude! You can trust Ahmadi. Why, he adores Martha's shadow!"

Jude said, "Sorry, but I'm not trusting my own shadow at the moment. However, if that's Ahmadi's story – "

"But it isn't. You've got it wrong," said Ben. "Ahmadi found the house shut up and came back to report. Then *I* went along and questioned the neighbours."

"Did you go to the house yourself?"

"What was the use? I took Ahmadi's word that Youssif's mule had gone. And though my Arabic is nothing to write home about, the people I spoke to certainly said he had planned to leave at dawn."

"Ah, but which dawn – this morning's or tomorrow's? You know they date their day differently."

"But if they meant tomorrow's, Youssif would still be there, and he could solve the mystery for us," Ben argued reasonably.

Jude nodded. "Always supposing the message which took Martha out was genuine," he said.

At that Dorrit blanched. "Jude, you're not suggesting someone *lured* her out? You don't think – ?" she pleaded.

173

He turned on her. "I'm not thinking. I'm doing," he said. "I'm finding Martha if it means turning the Quarter inside out. Come on, Ben – "

Dorrit followed them out. "You'll bring her back here? I'll have a bed ready for her. And – and everything," she called after them. But her words were drowned in the snarl of the engine of Jude's car.

Whenever Martha stirred or clapped her hands the predatory scurryings would stop as if in affronted surprise, only to begin again as soon as she was still. But though she knew the bold, the sane thing would be to patrol the floor from end to end and back again she could not make the initial effort, and stayed where she was, straining her ears for the first sound which would be different . . . human.

Yet when it came a long while later, though she would have sworn she was still wide-eyed and alert, her uneasy half-sleep heard it only as a new menace, a terrifying crescendo of all the rest.

She froze – not recognizing it for what it was – the thud of the ladderhead being readjusted against the flange on which it rested. Nor in the moment which followed did the terse voices from below reach her. But she was fully awake to the next sound. It was the unmistakable tread of feet on rungs. Someone, then, was mounting the ladder and would find her. But was it Ben in anxious search of her, or Hadrassi about his furtive affairs, never guessing she was here? And if it were Hadrassi – ?

But she was to be spared the full dread of that. Already there was the insistent thump of fists on the underside of the trapdoor; the creak of its reluctant yielding; a widening aperture lighted by the beam of a torch from below; then a silhouetted head and shoulders which could not be Hadrassi's, and then – arms into which she stumbled blindly, but which were not Ben's . . .

Jude held her close, crushing her to him as if she were a precious thing found, instead of the misguided meddler he must think her. Above her bent head he spoke her name – "Martha – !" and then was scolding, "You little fool. You little, little *beloved* fool!" – over and over, the endearment as emphatic as the blame.

Beloved . . . She heard it, marvelling, treasuring it, even if she must believe it only sprang from the edged reaction of his fears for her. Then Ben was there, climbing in over the edge of the trap, shining his torch and exclaiming, "Martha!" in his turn.

Jude released her and she put trembling hands to her hair and her flaming face. "H – how did you find me?" she asked shakily.

"By this. It was half buried under a little hillock of grain down below," Jude told her.

"My handkerchief? Oh – !" She took it from him, making nervous play with it to avoid meeting his eyes so soon after that "Beloved". "I must have dropped it when I came up here to find out how that pile of grain came to be there. But that was just after Youssif and Fatima left – hours ago. Or was it?" she appealed to both men. "Have I lost all count of time?"

Jude said, "It was long enough. It's close on midnight now."

"Yes, well – then the trapdoor slammed on me and I couldn't open it from this side. But I hoped you would find me sooner, if Ben got the note I left for him."

Ben nodded. "I got it all right. Only thing was, by the time I set hue-and-cry afoot for you, you had disappeared, and Youssif's neighbours assured me that he had left at dawn – this morning."

"Originally he had meant to, yes."

"Well, that seemed to make nonsense of your note, and

175

a search for you around here rather futile. You'd said that you had been called to Youssif's baby, not that he had fetched you himself. And as that was impossible if he had already gone away, nothing about the whole thing seemed to tie in. You've got Jude to thank for deciding to tear this area apart first before we began on the rest of the town in search of you."

Martha summoned a smile. "And here I was, all the time."

"And here you were indeed. What's your middle name – Sherlock, by any chance? Fancy your catching on to that pile of wheat"! Ben raised his torch and raked the granary from end to end with its beam. "All this, Chief! Where d'you suppose it all came from? And *whose* is it? It can't be Youssif's!"

Martha said quickly, "It isn't. Youssif told me before he left that he rented this place to Hadrassi the merchant, but that it was empty, and I don't think he was lying."

Ben and Jude looked at each other. "Hadrassi!" echoed Jude. "So this is where the old so-and-so has been cacheing the stuff away until he judged he could ask and get his own price for it!"

"But – packing it in, with Youssif knowing nothing about it? Oh, come again!" Ben scoffed.

"I don't know so much. If Youssif had had an inkling there was this lot literally under his own roof, he'd have stayed put. No, with no windows to the houses, these alleys and courts are as dead as graveyards at night, and I imagine that's when Hadrassi may have brought it, alone and probably by the single sackload, and using a rope-ladder of his own."

"But the trapdoor wasn't barred or locked!"

"Only this once, I should think. Perhaps on his last visit he had to skip in a hurry. In which case he'll be back, and I can hardly wait – Meanwhile, the top priority is to get Martha out of this and home. Lead the way down, will you, and show a light for her. Ready, Martha? Dorrit has a bed waiting for you, and Ben will take you straight there instead of to your own quarters."

Obediently Martha followed Ben through the trap, but turned on the ladder to face Jude. "But you're coming too?" she asked.

He crouched in the aperture just above. "Not yet," he said. "Ben can bring the car back for me at first light. But on the off-chance that friend Hadrassi may show up, I've quite a yearning to be here when he does. But, Martha – ?"

She searched his face for some clue to "Beloved". "Yes?" she said.

"Just – bless you for this night's work. But don't make a habit of being so catastrophe-prone in future. My nerves won't stand it." Momentarily his hand went to touch her cheek and to linger about the contour of her jaw. "Meanwhile, goodnight," he said. "If you need it, get Ben to give you something to help you sleep, and I'll see you in the morning. Wait for me."

It was not an order. Somehow he made "Wait for me" sound as if it were both a promise and the asking of a boon. . . .

When Martha woke the sun was high and Dorrit was at her bedside with a coffee-tray. Dorrit said, "This is the umpteenth time I've peeped at you, and not once have you stirred. Jude looked in at you too, and said to let you sleep on, and that he'd be back – "

Jude. Martha rubbed sleep from her eyes and made an effort to sort dreams from reality. "I must get up," she said, throwing back the covers.

Balancing the tray on one hand, Dorrit promptly replaced them. "I thought you'd want to be up to see

Jude, so I've had Saluma bring you a change of clothes and some make-up and your toilet things. But I haven't run your bath yet, because you're to have your coffee first. Is it all right?" she added as she set the tray across Martha's knees.

Martha looked with pleasure at the fringed gingham traycloth with its matching napkin, the gleaming china of the breakfast set which had been her own gift to Dorrit, the thin crisp toast and the rolled butter, and compared it with the rough-and-ready service the girl would have regarded as "good enough" a few months earlier.

"It's delightful," Martha told her, adding as she poured coffee. "You'd better put me in the rest of the picture, hadn't you? What happened after Jude stayed at the granary? Did Hadrassi turn up there after all?"

"He hadn't, when Ben went back for Jude as soon as it was light, and Jude was hopping mad, because he wanted to catch him redhanded. Anyway, they went together to rout him out and they gave him the works – requisitioned the lot in the Sheikh's name and suggested Hadrassi might care to leave town before the news got round the markets. He tried to bluff, though of course he couldn't, and they made him admit that Youssif hadn't had a clue. But imagine, Martha," Dorrit's eyes rounded indignantly, "Jude calculates the bread potential of all that grain the old devil had hoarded was enough to feed every child in Taroued for weeks!"

"That's how it looked to me. Not to mention the few hundred rats it seemed to be nourishing last night," shuddered Martha.

"I know. You poor thing – I'd have *died*. Funny that, come to think of it – the way any normal female's reaction to vermin is that she'd far rather meet a herd of rhino head-on. Well, that's Hadrassi, that was. But what about the other news? I suppose in the general carry-on last night, no one got around to telling you that either?"

"What other news?"

"Why, that yesterday in Bab Magreb the Sheikh volunteered to play ball to the tune of all the funds Jude estimates Taroued heeds for food relief between now and next harvest!"

"At last? What a wonderful triumph for Jude!" breathed Martha.

"And how!" Dorrit agreed. "Apparently, on the strength of the first of his oil royalties, the old boy admitted that he could well afford it. And with the Company getting into really big production next year, and work and money beginning to flow, Ben and Jude say it can't ever be as bad again. And that's a funny thing, too," she added, and stopped.

"What is?"

"Well, that though I've hated this place like nobody's business, and especially before you came, now it's going to be like leaving an exciting book half finished when Ben and I go and, believe it or not, I've begun to feel quite cheated of the rest!"

"You'll have to come back," said Martha.

Dorrit shook her head. "Maybe we shall. But coming back is never the same, even if we could lug Martha Ann out here, which we couldn't for ages yet!"

Martha puckered a brow. "Martha Ann? Am I tuned in to the right channel?"

Dorrit dimpled. "Michael Jude as was! It's just that last night Ben and I decided we ought to budget for the fifty-fifty chance that he might be a girl, not minding which really, as long as he-cum-she turns up in due season." As she spoke she relieved Martha of the tray and was on her way out, promising to run the bath, when she stopped and turned.

"Know what?" she said. "I've just remembered it's Stores Day at Base, and I promised Ben I wouldn't serve tinned mulligatawny again if David brought anything different in, this trip. But if I don't get to the head of the queue, those Base chefs will snaffle the lot. So would you mind if I shot over in the car this morning? Anything you want while I'm there?"

"Anything I want?"

"*Stores*, dear!" Dorrit grinned exaggerated patience with Martha's absent tone. "Pins, pineapple chunks, face-powder, detergents – *you* know!"

"Oh – Why, no, thanks, I don't think so. Are you going now?"

"Well, not straight away. I'll wait until you're clothed and in your right mind to cope with Jude when he comes. Why did he make such a thing of coming back to see you anyway, do you suppose?"

"I – don't know," said Martha, feeling a prick of guilt when Dorrit nodded and took the half-truth at its face value, but knowing she had needed to make it her talisman against dreams and the sweet promise she had read into Jude's "Wait for me".

In their small community no one stood on the ceremony of waiting for admittance. So that when Jude came on foot, while Martha's ears were alert for the sound of his car, he was in the living room, closing the door behind him with his foot, almost before she knew he was there.

She started up to face him, taken off guard. *"Oh – !"*

For a moment he stood, leaning slightly back against the door and looking at her hungrily. Then in a single movement he lunged forward, his arms went wide in invitation, and when she ran into them with another little

180

choked cry, they locked about her, and his searching lips found hers, gently at first and then in mounting demand of the response her own gave willingly back . . . and back again.

While it lasted, they were at one in ecstasy, in the utter rapture of sharing a need, a hunger, which only the urgency of their kisses and their murmured endearments could make eloquent enough. But just so, unbidden passion had sparked between them once before, and when at last Jude held her gently off from him, she saw his worried eyes and was ashamed.

"This time, you – wanted that? It was for real? For keeps? For – me?" he pleaded.

That he should need to ask! "From me to you, it was real that – other time," she told him.

The hands which had rested lightly on her shoulders tightened to a grip that was a sweet agony. "No," he said. "If it had been, you couldn't have brushed me off as you did, made me feel as if I'd committed rapine, as if I'd despoiled your dreams!"

"I didn't! You hadn't!" she protested. "But I thought you were kissing me for no deeper reason than that I was – there. After all, you had forbidden me to cherish dreams and even memories, and I knew you saw love only as a curb on you, an intrusion you wouldn't tolerate. I believe it was only that night that I had admitted to myself that I loved you and knew I ached to be in your arms. But I couldn't bear – couldn't *bear*, don't you understand? – for you to make love to me without meaning anything by it. As – as men do," she added lamely.

"And as women, never?"

"Oh, some can and do. Naomi, for one, I think. She took a pride in being able to kiss and move on without any regrets. And she warned me – if I needed warning! – that you and she were cut to much the same pattern, the only difference being that she rode away to another affair, and you back to your work."

"Naomi!" Jude's tone dismissed her. "But you? I could kiss you as I did that night – with everything I had – and could still convey nothing of what I hoped I was telling you, asking of you? Oh, Martha, was my love-making really as inarticulate as that?"

Her colour flamed. "Not while – That is, I *wanted* to hope, and for a moment or two I let myself. But I thought I daren't, if I wasn't to get hurt all over again. And then, afterwards, when you backed out by asking me to realize that you were only 'a very ordinary man', I was sure I understood what you meant by that, and I could have died of shame."

"A very ordinary man!" He made much of each word. "But, my darling, that was my way of telling you how very ordinary I'd just realized I was! That I'd fallen in love, just like the next chap, that I couldn't and didn't want to ride roughshod over it, as I'd always told myself I must; that I loved *you* and wanted you to know it, regardless."

"Yet you let me go so easily! Why?"

"Because of that sneer of yours about 'co-operation' which I took to be your idea of tact, your way of telling me you had only been embracing your memories, not me at all. Which wasn't much encouragement to ask any more of you when I could offer you so little in return."

"Why, what would you have asked of me?"

"Too much. All I could have said would have been something like – 'I love you. Be loyal to me, Martha; work with me; keep your heart whole for me, as mine will always be whole for you.' But I wouldn't have added, 'Share my life with me, marry me,' for I felt I hadn't the right – then."

"If you had said the rest, it would have been enough – "

"Wanting you and respecting you as I did and do – no. Though I know I'd have been tempted to try again later, if Ryder hadn't re-erupted into your life the next day."

"His coming meant nothing to me. It wouldn't have done, even if I hadn't been all yours by then. But I was. And if you had ever said anything of – all that, I'd have told you yes . . . and yes . . . and *yes*!"

"I wonder? Don't you remember that after Ryder had been booted out and you had convinced me you were cured of him, even though you conceded you and I were still friends, you didn't let me get a mile nearer than that to you, to the real you, the you of that night in Bab Magreb? Well, did you?" he urged gently of her silence.

She shook her head. "No. But you were being so analytical and cool and judicial that I was afraid."

"Afraid of *me*?"

"Of letting you guess how much I cared, if your feelings stopped short at friendship. And besides, there was Naomi – No, wait" – she forestalled his convulsive movement – "I think I knew she meant nothing to you. But at the Base party, when Nick Murray fetched you to Dorrit, I'd already been in search of you and had seen you by your car and Naomi with you in your arms. I didn't wait. I couldn't. I just ran, thinking, 'With Naomi – like that tonight. And with me – in the same way – in Bab Magreb!' And I vowed, 'Not with me again, ever! *Not with me*.' "

At that Jude put her gently into Dorrit's chaise-longue and sat on the foot-rest, holding both her hands.

"Listen," he said. "Naomi was quite a girl. She had zing, she had glamour by the three bagsful – and still had as little for me as I had for her, if only because we had taken cold-blooded measure of each other quite early on."

"But you had gone out with her?"

"Escorted her to parties in people's quarters and to the odd dinner date in Bab Magreb to which she wasn't above inviting herself, yes."

"And you had kissed her before?"

"That too. Because she was the type to think her technique was slipping if one didn't. But that night we clinched for a different reason. You could say it was partly my despair of you, craving the company of her despair of the little which, in her heart, she knew she had left from the countless affairs which had died on her here. I'd gone out to the car to see how it was placed for our getting away, and she followed me out. She had spent too much of her evening at the bar; she was a little maudlin and more than a little in need of reassurance. So I did my best to give it to her in the kind of terms she understood. On her last night here – was that so wrong?"

Martha said slowly, "If it did anything for her, I'm glad you did. She was jaunty and debonair enough the next day. But we talked before she left, and I realized then how very alone she was and always had been."

"Did you tell her you had witnessed her dramatic leavetaking of me?"

"I didn't have to. She had seen me, and she had guessed I needed warning against falling in love with you. In fact, her last word to me as she boarded her plane was 'Don't!'" Martha smiled.

"Advice which, if I'm to believe you, came too late?" Jude queried.

"I've told you, a lot too late!"

"And now you understand I was only going through the motions with Naomi, you aren't saying 'Not with me' any more? But what do you find to love in me, Martha – tell me?" he urged.

She laughed. "You shouldn't expect a list. But – these.

184

You – " She indicated his hands, his bulk. "Your single-mindedness, your fairness, your compassion. What do you love in me?"

"Everything you are. Not to mention this . . . and this . . . and this – " The kisses with which he pointed his meaning left her in no doubt of it before he sat back, his eyes a little grave.

He said, "I'm asking you to marry me now because I can't help myself. Wanting you and needing to protect you as I do, it's as inevitable as tomorrow's sun-up that I should. But since I told myself I hadn't the right to ask you, nothing has really changed for me. You realize that?"

She bent forward to cup his face between her hands. "I realize you're telling me *you* haven't changed. But when did I ever ask that?" she said.

He turned his lips against her palm. "You haven't, bless you. But you know what I mean? There's work in plenty for me here still, but a year or two hence – perhaps less, perhaps more – Taroued will be all set to solve its own problems. And then – well, do you remember my telling you once that whether or not I succeeded or failed here, there would always be other Taroueds for me? And there will be, marriage notwithstanding. Are you prepared to face that?"

"I should think less of you if you didn't ask it of me. And with you, I can face anything," she told him.

"Even if it's not always possible for us to be together? If there should be times when I can't have you along, places where I have to go ahead, leaving you to follow?"

"Even that. It's happening to wives every day and all over the world, and the lonely times would only be the price I'd be willing to pay for the privilege of loving you as you are, not wanting you different."

He looked at her tenderly. "I always knew you had bags of courage, and if I had dared to hope you had all that wisdom and generosity as well, I needn't have wasted the time I did," he said. "But now, how soon will you marry me and where? Shall we bring Padre Dobson up to Base or go down to Bab Magreb?"

Martha said happily, "I don't mind. Anywhere."

"Then we'll make it Bab Magreb. It has a spectre or two to be laid. Do you want banns, or shall I get a special licence?"

"Banns, please. I love them. They're such proud, two-before-the-world things."

"You shall have your banns, and we'll fix a day before Ben and Dorrit leave. What are they going to say about all this, by the way?"

"I don't think they have a clue, so they'll get a shock, and we shall be at the receiving end of a lot of the 'We told you so's' that happily married people are always so glib with. But I can face that, can't you?"

For answer Jude would have taken her into his arms again. But she held him off. "One thing – did you really only let me come to Taroued because I happened to speak enough Arabic to get by?" she asked.

His eyes narrowed with laughter as he gathered her to him.

"Fishing? Suppose you try to guess," he said.

Mills & Boon's Paperbacks

MAY

THE VELVET SPUR BY JANE ARBOR

The last request that Maria's mother had made was that she should go to Corsica to meet the aunt she had never seen. Maria had often wondered why her mother had never spoken of the home and family she had left when she married an Englishman. Gian Laurent and his brother Orso might be able to explain the mystery to her. But why did her aunt so strongly disapprove of them?

THE FIRES OF TORRETTA BY IRIS DANBURY

Rosamund was furious when, inspecting the villa which her employer had rented for his stay in Sicily, she found a strange man apparently in occupation there. Brent Stanton was no Adonis, she thought, and his hectoring, overbearing manner added nothing to his appearance. Yet Erica, her employer's daughter, and the beautiful Adriana Mandelli made it only too clear that they found Brent irresistible. Could Rosamund be mistaken?

THE WAY OF A TYRANT BY ANNE HAMPSON

Because Jane desired a little mastery in her husband she turned down the gentle and accommodating Scott Kingsley. But four years later, when she went to Barbados, Jane met Scott again – by no means the man she had known. Dictatorial and overbearing, contemptuous of women, he had no longer any desire to marry her. And now, of course, Jane had to fall madly in love with him . . .

RUN FROM THE WIND BY REBECCA STRATTON

Laura had heard so much about the little French village of St. Louis les Bigots from her Uncle John that she had always longed to visit it – and now she was here at last. But what was the mystery surrounding Uncle John, and what had he done to make the villagers hate his memory? And why was Laura so anxious to clear his name, particularly where Jean-Pierre Hervé was concerned?

THE GEMEL RING BY BETTY NEELS

"I hope you will believe me when I say that I dislike you more than anyone else I know," Charity Dawson told that annoying Dutchman Everard van Tijlen. Perhaps it was just as well that he didn't take her words too seriously!

20p net each

Mills & Boon's Paperbacks

MAY (contd.)

RACHEL TREVELLYAN BY ANNE MATHER

The arrogant Luis Martinez, Marqués de Mendao, made it clear that all he felt for Rachel was contempt. Did it matter that she seemed unable to convince him that he was wrong about her? And what about Malcolm's feelings?

THE LOVE THEME BY MARGARET WAY

Damian St. Clair was notorious for his success with women – and for sidestepping the issue of marriage. It was important for Siri to succeed at her audition with him. How would she make out with the famous Damian as a singer – and as a woman?

THE FIELDS OF HEAVEN BY ANNE WEALE

When Imelda opened her antique shop, Charles Wingfield was one of those who expressed their doubts about her capacity to handle the venture. She assured him, "I can't be duped by a phoney person," and he replied, "Not as a dealer. As a girl you might be." Could he be right?

THE TARTAN TOUCH BY ISOBEL CHACE

From being the prim daughter of the Manse, within a few days, amazingly, Kirsty found herself on the other side of the world, in the Australian Outback, as the wife "in name only" of Andrew Fraser. It was going to be difficult enough to adjust even before she realized that her husband was in love with another woman . . .

LOVE IN HIGH PLACES BY JANE BEAUFORT

American heiress Lou Morgan was travelling round the high spots of Europe in search of a titled husband – and she found him, in the attractive person of Baron Alex von Felden. Unfortunately the Baron fell in love with the wrong girl – with Lou's penniless little companion. Valentine Brown . . .

20p net each

Mills & Boon's Paperbacks

JUNE

MOON OVER THE ALPS BY ESSIE SUMMERS

Penny had been sure that Charles's friendship for her was something more than a holiday romance, but he had made it clear it wasn't. So Penny found herself a new life, on a remote sheep station in the New Zealand Alps, to try to forget. It was unfortunate that she should have chosen the one place in the world where this would prove most difficult.

THE KING OF SPADES BY KATRINA BRITT

When Sara Everette met the fascinating Armand Romonte whom she considered to be responsible for the death of her friend she decided that she hated him and would make him pay for his actions. But she was to find that hatred can be akin to love.

PALACE OF THE POMEGRANATE BY VIOLET WINSPEAR

Life had not been an easy ride for Grace Wilde and she had every reason to be distrustful of men. Then, in the Persian desert, she fell into the hands of another man, Kharim Khan, who was different from any other man she had met ...

LOGAN'S ISLAND BY MARY WIBBERLEY

Helen had inherited an island off the coast of Brazil – jointly with an unknown man called Jake Logan. Its name – Island of Storms – just about summed up the wildly antagonistic relationship that promptly developed between the two of them!

PINK SANDS BY WYNNE MAY

Much as she enjoyed working for Sir Basil Harvester, Barbara had never intended to fall in love with his son, Gregory. But then Sir Basil's glamorous goddaughter Reina, and Barbara's former boy-friend Rod, saw to it that nothing serious should come of the affair anyway!

20p net each

Mills & Boon's Paperbacks

JUNE (contd.)

A TIME TO LOVE BY RUTH CLEMENCE

Angie had had no intention of falling in love with Pablo Pendleton – but in spite of herself she had. For Pablo was her sister Netta's property – and even though Pablo seemed to have no scruples about flirting with her, how could Angie hurt her sister by encouraging him?

IF DREAMS CAME TRUE BY ROBERTA LEIGH

Briony loved Christopher Clayton, but it was his brother she married – a marriage of convenience to suit his ambition and her financial needs. Would her career as a dancer be enough to make up for the complete lack of love in her life?

THE MAGIC OF LIVING BY BETTY NEELS

When Arabella was involved in a road crash in Holland, it seemed providential that the first person to arrive on the scene should be Doctor Gideon van der Vorst. But as she became more and more involved with the doctor, Arabella began to wonder if providence had, after all, known what it was doing!

MOON WITHOUT STARS BY ANNE HAMPSON

Jill found her life serene on the South African farm owned by her brother and his wife – until the advent of the superior Dean Lester, a timber planter, who had taken over Nyala Mount, a neighbouring property. It took the arrival of the glamorous Sylvia de Courcy to make Jill realise she didn't dislike Dean any more . . .

TIME SUSPENDED BY JEAN S. MACLEOD

Ruth had to go to Antigua to search for her missing sister, and a lot was going to depend on a man called Logan Carse. Logan, she was told, "could be a gentleman or a pirate". If he turned out to be a pirate, which seemed likely, how could she manage to cope with him?

20p net each

MILLS & BOON FIESTA!

25 Favourite titles now available once again

MILLS & BOON are bringing 25 of their favourite titles back into print. If you would like to obtain any of these titles please contact your local stockist or in case of difficulty please use the order form overleaf for your requirements.

FREE! YOUR COPY OF OUR MAGAZINE OF MILLS & BOON ROMANCES

Complete the coupon below and send it to MILLS & BOON READER SERVICE, P.O. Box 236, 14 Sanderstead Road, S. Croydon, Surrey CR2 OYG we will gladly send you, post free, your own copy of our magazine – "Happy Reading" together with our complete stock list of over 400 Mills & Boon romances.

LOOK OUT FOR THESE TITLES

☐ THE SEA CHANGE — Catherine Airlie
☐ LAKE OF SHADOWS — Jane Arbor
☐ THE WHITE OLEANDER (Nurse Laurie) — Kathryn Blair
☐ STORMY HAVEN — Rosalind Brett
☐ ACCOMPANIED BY HIS WIFE — Mary Burchell
☐ THE HOSPITAL OF FATIMA — Isobel Chace
☐ AT THE VILLA MASSINA — Celine Conway
☐ THE TIMBER MAN — Joyce Dingwell
☐ A CHANGE FOR CLANCY — Amanda Doyle
☐ SONG OF SUMMER (Doctor's Orders) — Eleanor Farnes
☐ DOCTOR IN BRAZIL (Truant Heart) — Patricia Fenwick
☐ SURGERY IN THE HILLS — Ivy Ferrari
☐ YOUNG BAR — Jane Fraser
☐ APPLE ISLAND — Gladys Fullbrook
☐ LOVE FROM A SURGEON — Elizabeth Gilzean
☐ CHERRY BLOSSOM CLINIC — Elizabeth Hunter
☐ ISLAND IN THE DAWN — Averil Ives
☐ THE TAMING OF LAURA — Rachel Lindsay
☐ CRANE CASTLE — Jean S. MacLeod
☐ NEW DREAMS FOR OLD — Jane Marnay
☐ DEAR DRAGON — Sara Seale
☐ THE CAPTAIN'S TABLE — Alex Stuart
☐ HIS SERENE MISS SMITH — Essie Summers
☐ GIRL ABOUT TOWN — Anne Weale
☐ THE TURQUOISE SEA — Hilary Wilde

All priced at 20p. See over for handy order form. Please tick titles required.